The Lowlife

The Lowlife

Alexander Baron

Black Spring Press

Published in 2010 by Black Spring Press Ltd
Curtain House
134–146 Curtain Road
London
EC2A 3AR

www.blackspringpress.co.uk

First published in Great Britain by William Collins & Co. Ltd, London 1963

ISBN: 978-0-948238-45-1

A full CIP record for this book is available from the British Library

Cover design Ken Leeder

Typeset in Calisto by Dexter Haven Associates Ltd, London
Printed and bound in Great Britain by CPI Cox & Wyman, Reading

Also by Alexander Baron

From the City, From the Plough (1948)

There's No Home (1950)

Rosie Hogarth (1951)

With Hope, Farewell (1952)

The Human Kind (1953)

The Golden Princess (1954)

Queen of the East (1956)

Seeing Life (1958)

Strip Jack Naked (1966)

King Dido (1969)

The In-Between Time (1971)

Gentle Folk (1976)

Franco Is Dying (1977)

CONTENTS

Introduction

IAIN SINCLAIR

We live at a time when the pre-forgotten seek out the reforgotten, the old ones, hoping to verify a mythical past. Alexander Baron, when I visited him (with the film-maker Chris Petit) in the tranquillity of his Golders Green retirement, knew very well that the game had changed: he no longer had the publishers' phone numbers, but he kept on writing. That's what he did. What he had always done, since he returned from the war; a D-Day corporal, a former Communist. 'A firebrand', he called himself, 'an extremist'. Why on earth would we want to talk to him? His books had drifted out of print. Even copies of his first big successes, *From the City, From the Plough* (1948), a novel which ran through countless editions, had to be searched out on market stalls or in Isle of Thanet charity pits. Baron's Golders Green, like the Mexican border town in Jim Thompson's *The Getaway*, was a reservation of the living dead. Memory men, indulging a non-specific pain, traced the trajectory of sentiment as far as they could comfortably take it, to the edge of the abyss: Whitechapel.

We took Baron back to Cheshire Street, to Hare Marsh, the location for *King Dido* (1969), a fierce fable in which a working man rages against his inevitable fate, the taint in stone; the way that certain areas defy redemption. The elderly author, unpublished since 1979, when his Spanish novel, *Franco Is Dying*, met with the indifference that seems to be the lot of any awkward cuss who refuses to step aside when his number's up, was bemused to find himself transported to an unconvincing but oddly familiar set. With his stocky build, silvered hair, fists bunched in the pockets of a white raincoat, he reminded Petit of the actor Lino Ventura in a underworld flick by Jean-Pierre Melville. Baron was physically strong but out of sync with present dereliction and neglect, the corrugated fence, the piles of smouldering rubbish, the feral dogs. To regress, to dredge up reminiscences of post-war Hackney, the family home, months of wandering the streets like a sleepwalker, was visibly stressful. He faced the cameras, square on, but his eyes moved away, tracking a palpable absence.

Something had gone badly wrong. The novels, when Baron discussed them with one of the new generation who found their way to his house—the novelist John Williams, or the researchers Jeb Nichols and Lorraine Morley (*Other Words*, December 1988)—were written by a doppelganger, a cocky pretender who shared the old man's name. 'You've stirred up memories there,' he would say. This was a *mensch*, modest, soft-spoken, generous with his time. A man who had outlived his expectations. There were no comebacks on the horizon, but Baron's books, so the youthful pilgrims insisted, lived on in the perpetual present of achieved and transformed experience. Reservoirs of darkness can never be dispersed. The Hare Marsh pub, outside which Dido Peach fights, emerged with the passage of time as the Carpenter's Arms, a command post for the Kray twins; the backwater from which they set out on the night that Jack 'The Hat' McVitie was killed. Violence feeds on acoustic echoes, fictional templates.

Baron was a true Londoner, which is to say a second-generation immigrant, a professional stranger; the confrontations of urban life were always a major part of his project. His novels are enactments of placed (rather than displaced) autobiography. Favoured geographical zones represent stages in the evolution of the author's sensibility. *King Dido* is Whitechapel, the bloody theatre of survival; the microclimate from which the disenfranchised newcomer has to escape. Aspirant Hackney tolerates the well-crafted fiction of Baron's maturity. Golders Green is the serene garden, the final reservation from which all the mistakes, loves and dramas can be recalled, re-imagined, appeased.

Hackney was where Baron returned when he was demobbed. To his mother's house. A period of wandering the streets, meditative traverses, gave him the time to notice the minute particulars of a ravished landscape, the scams and hustles, the culture shifts. Years later, in 1963, sifting those post-war memories, he would craft *The Lowlife*, his delirious Hackney novel. 'A writer's job,' Baron told Jeb Nichols, 'is to be the spectator who hopes he can see more of the game and try to make sense of it.'

The wonder of *The Lowlife* is that it does justice to a place of so many contradictions, disguises, deceptions, multiple identities. Hackney, I had thought, was defined by being indefinable. A fistful of mercury. Shape it and it spills. A logging of Kingsland Road, which I attempted in *Lights Out for the Territory* (a book of speculative London essays), was redundant before I reached Dalston Junction. Graffiti, as I copied them into a notebook, were overpainted; the heavy drench of jerk chicken giving way to the scented fug of Kurdish football clubs. Balkan refugees punting contraband cigarettes blocked my view of a voodoo boutique that was doomed before I could finish counting the shrunken skulls. An old-time manufacturer of bespoke dressing-gowns (think David Kossoff) lived on as a faded sign, partly obscured by a swiveling surveillance camera on a tall pole. Time is thinner (and faster) now. More text, less meaning. *The Lowlife*, with the lean and disciplined structure of old-time social realist television, captures the moment of transition. The known is still known—market gardens, brickworks, oily-fingered industry—but the new life, brought by the West Indians, Bangladeshis, is recognised early, and celebrated.

Harryboy Boas, a gambler and sometime Hofmann presser, lives in a boarding-house (timid/aggressive landlord skulking like a rat in the basement), on the hinge of Dalston and Stoke Newington; between the frenzy of Ridley Road Market and the hushed Hasidic enclave to the north. Harry has a privileged sense of history: as personal experience. He knows that Hackney isn't, properly speaking, the East End. Nobody stays there. It's a staging post on the journey to respectability. (*EastEnders*, the TV soap, accurately replicates the physical outline of squares and pubs that can be found in the borough, but its fabulous demographics—mouthy geezers with a graveyard pallor, nightclub speculators, blacks and Asians as token frame-fillers— belong much further out. In Essex. Romford, Hornchurch, Upminster.)

Harry is detached, an observer. He's damaged; compensating for events in his own past which have left him with a nagging sense of loss. He lives in an amnesiac daze, a willed forgetting: existential burn-out in the shadow of the Holocaust. Nothing to be done and he's doing it on a daily basis. He has his analgesic rituals: the heavy lunch, long afternoons reading and dozing on the bed, the prostitute, the good cigar. Gambling is risk, inevitable loss. Necessary punishment. It is his only connection to the life of the city, the mob. The rigorous scholarship with which Harryboy chases his fancies, three-legged dogs and hobbled nags, is religious. He is a righteous man studying the Torah of the Tote. Temporary wealth, the wad that spoils the hang of a good suit, must be rapidly dispersed, recycled; converted into secondhand literature. Conspicuous charity, hits of sensual pleasure, return Harryboy to the Zen calm of having nothing, no possessions, no attachments, no unfulfilled ambitions.

The Lowlife moves at a pace. The mundane domesticity of Harryboy's boarding-house totters on the brink of a Gothic abyss, the half-remembered horrors of Whitechapel and the river. If he should falter, lose faith, hit a bad run at the track, he could be sucked into the swamp, the Jack London nightmare. He would join the animals, fighting for a crust. In one vivid episode, Harry takes an excursion to the lower depths: he's toying with respectability, an investment in a slum property. He wins a house, a terrace of houses, on a cut of the cards; then loses everything to an Indian in a Cable Street dive: 'a smell in the café which was like asthma cigarettes'. Alexander Baron forsees Peter Rachman: the treaty of convenience between prostitution, dope, bricks and mortar. The Hackney gambler is advised by Marcia, a tart he sometimes visits: 'Slums. You buy them for the last five years before clearance and stuff them with niggers... You could clean up, Harry. You don't need much capital, you can buy a house for two hundred.' The spit-on-the-palm economics of the city are revealed. Harry's unobtrusive, semi-detached life, weeks lying on a bed working his way through Zola, is tenable because another place, the nightland of illicit pleasures, is a 73 bus ride away.

Many East London Jewish writers have left accounts of these transits, shuttling between home (the ghetto) and the lawless cellar (gambling, booze, miscegenation). Bernard Kops in *The World is a Wedding* (1963) links the claustrophobia of family life in Stepney Green with the liberties of Soho bohemia. Roland Camberton, in his Hackney novel *Rain on the Pavements* (1951), sends his young men (arguing about literature and politics—like Harold Pinter's gang in *The Dwarfs*) to Italian cafés where they smoke, discuss Eliot and write bad poetry. Camberton was one of a number of working-class writers patronised by the publisher John Lehmann. The book jacket for Camberton's novel featured a Neo-Romantic composition by John Minton, an independently wealthy cruiser who taught at the Royal College of Art. Minton's Hackney could be anywhere, a generically dingy streetscape through which L.S. Lowry smudges drag their sodden banners. Lehmann's promising young men were supposed to act as salaried spies, Mass-Observers sent out to document the bizarre habits of the proles.

Alexander Baron was never part of that crowd. He met Ashley Smith, author of the day-in-the-life reportage *A City Stirs* (1939), and he knew people who knew Whitechapel authors of an earlier generation, Simon Blumenfeld and Willy Goldman. But it wasn't his business to satirise or complain. Novels dealing with group dynamics, the community, gave way, at the time of *The Lowlife*, to the psychopathology of one recalcitrant individual: a self-punishing moralist, a gambler. Harryboy Boas chases fate as a way of divorcing himself from tradition, religion, family expectations. He's an elective lowlife. An unachieved elitist. An autodidact. And therefore a non-writing writer, an artist of the city, trained to appreciate subtle shifts in mood and weather. Harry, gazing out of his high window, is eager to welcome the next wave of immigrants, but wary of the first signs of the great American consumer push: retail conformity, the suits and cars and sounds that East End hoods customised in their bid for the violence franchise.

British movies, aping the hardboiled style, imported Hollywood heavies to play Jewish wide boys: Richard Widmark, in Jules Dassin's version of Gerald Kersh's *Night and the City*. But the gambling-fever novel traces its lineage to Dostoevsky. It's a well-tested device: the outsider, the believer in arcane systems, divorces himself from righteous society, begs, cheats, lies, steals, subverts every taboo. Revengers set out on his trail. He runs. He tries to borrow. He confronts the mobsters, the professionals of hurt who are out to damage or destroy him. It's a standard riff, a way of giving tension a structure. Think of Anthony Newley, the sleazy, sweating, chain-smoking clipjoint MC in Ken Hughes's film *The Small World of Sammy Lee* (1962). He races from Soho to the family shop in Whitechapel; to his brother, Warren Mitchell. Soliciting straight money that can soon be bent, burnt, blown away. Think of James Caan in Karel Reisz's film *The Gambler* (1975).

Back in the Sixties, it was Reisz's translation of Alan Sillitoe's *Saturday Night and Sunday Morning* that helped to marginalise the London lowlife novel. Suddenly the north was sexy. Nottingham, Rotherham, Liverpool, Blackpool: exotic, unknown and interchangeable. Cobbles, canals, industry. Horny-handed toilers with bicycles. Girls (RADA-trained) who couldn't cope with contraception. Oxford graduates, frequently gay or bisexual—Lindsay Anderson, Tony Richardson, John Schlesinger—dusted down the Lehmann trope. London fiction moved away from the Jewish working class (Baron,

Emanuel Litvinoff, Bernard Kops) to those who could talk up the changes, soft-sell the Swinging City. Photographers, pill poppers, property sharks.

The standard gambling novel or film depends on clocks. Phone calls. The cigarette lit from the dying butt. Frantic moves within an ever-tighter urban labyrinth: Gerald Kersh's *Night and the City* (1939), Robert Westerby's *Wide Boys Never Work* (1937). There's a firm structure and a liquid topography. But that isn't Baron's technique. He is so solidly grounded in place, in workaday Hackney. He runs a double narrative, the madness of the track and the betting shop interwoven with the history of a dysfunctional family (suburban ambitions reduced to the declining no-man's-land of Dalston). The child of this family becomes Harryboy's own 'lost' son. Characteristically, Baron spurns the grand finale, the eye that is to be sacrificed to save the child's sight. 'My great gesture fell as flat as all my other great plans.' The Russian novel of doomed souls is therefore reduced to an East London rag-trade copy. There was talk, according to Baron, who had good showbiz connections, about *The Lowlife* being optioned as a film; a vehicle for Harry H. Corbett, the young Steptoe. Comedic/sentimental script by Simpson and Galton? It never happened.

When I pitched out on a Camden Passage bookstall in the mid-Seventies, a speed-freak friend of Malcolm McLaren, who had grown up in the streets Baron describes so lovingly, told me that I should read this 'amazing' book, *The Lowlife*. He was, as usual, quite right. It was as if a direct descendant of Harryboy Boas, a runner, chaser of rumours, a hand-to-mouth man with a powerful appetite for literature and gossip, was recommending the autobiography he would never get around to writing. I picked up the Collins first edition (I don't remember seeing any other) within a few days. The runner talked so fast, quarrelled, embraced, argued, he must have done his reading on the wing: as he jogged between appointments. His taste was excellent. He puffed Colin MacInnes (*Absolute Beginners*), Michael Moorcock, Gerald Kersh, James Curtis. And he led me, with *The Lowlife*, to one of the best fictions, the truest accounts of the borough in which I had lived for ten years. I'm delighted to borrow, now, the runner's belted herringbone coat, to draw deep on his cigarette and to make his pitch. Here it is, the book, the place, the story. Enjoy.

Hackney, 2010

The Lowlife

CHAPTER ONE

One day, when I have got a few hundred pounds together, I will take a boat to the Canaries. I'll look around, and settle in on one of the smaller islands; somewhere out of the way. On four pounds a week, they tell me, you can live like a lord. A thousand would keep me for over four years.

Four years. A lifetime nowadays. We should have such luck.

I will read and swim, loaf about. No one will interfere, no one will judge me. If they drop that big cookie I can always go down to the beach and swim out into the warm sea till I can't swim any more.

Perfect.

All I need is a few hundred pounds.

My name is Harryboy Boas. (Bo-as, two syllables, please.) At the moment I have thirty pounds in the world. But I face the future with confidence. The dogs are running at White City tonight. In the third there is an animal, which, I heard this morning…Ah, I should have such luck. But a man can dream. I bother no one.

My story starts one night last year. It didn't seem a night different from any other. We are carried to the grave on a stream of dead days and nights. We live them and forget them. Yet who knows on which dead day or night a terrible change can come into a life? A disease starts. The seeds of a crisis, a disaster, a great joy, are sown. At the time we are aware of nothing. I didn't know that night. I went round to my sister Debbie. How could I know what was coming to me?

Debbie lives in Finchley, the smart part. Finchley, as few people know, is one of the millionaire quarters of London. There are roads in Finchley that make Kensington look poor. Houses at forty thousand, three-car garages (Rolls, Sonny's Jag and Mummy's shopping Dauphine), driveways, grounds front and rear, and butlers. Not that Debbie married so high. A fifteen-thousand-pound house and a Spanish couple to look after it is all she's got, poor girl. All right, so she hasn't done so bad. When she married Gus in the third year of the war, he was a boy without money, only a medical certificate to say the army didn't want him, and an ambition to make a book. So a book he made, and in a modest way, he hasn't done so badly. When did a bookie starve?

He is a good fellow, Gus. He didn't marry Deb for her money. Money in our family? Nor for her good looks. Debbie was always a fat girl, with a face so helpless and gentle it breaks your heart. He was fond of her. He liked the girl. It happens sometimes. With a good heart he married the girl, and I'm glad to say he got a happy marriage as a reward. Happy, that means no trouble, a good home, a yes-wife who is also a good cook. Peace to come home to. And three daughters. Terrible girls. All thin, all snooty, all the sort that flute 'Mummy' and 'Daddy' in high-class accents; they kiss Mummy and Daddy and feel a little more ashamed of them every year. Of their old man's bankroll they are not ashamed at all. For my nieces I feel no affection. God knows, I believe in family affection. I hunger for it. Shouldn't we, Debbie and I, after what happened?

Debbie, bless her heart, I love with an ache. We never talked together. We never had what they call a relationship. Strangers, always. But I look at her, and I know all about Debbie, and I think dumb Debbie, with her cow eyes, knows all about me. I think she cries sometimes for her no-good brother. We pity each other and say nothing.

I went round there that night, and not a bad word was said till after supper. This is a big point for Gus. I told you, he is a good man. Life Governor of hospitals. A name for generosity. He grunts something that sounds like a greeting, goes behind the bar (this is a semi-circular bar, all glass in front, lit from beneath, with richly coloured Venetian glasses on shelves. Very pretty. Behind the barman are the shelves of bottles, and behind the bottles is a big mirror) and pours me a whisky that would knock down a carthorse. He gives it to me, picks up his own and says, 'Cheers.' That's all. He must have been bursting, but he kept his anger in.

Debbie, dear Debbie, just comes out into the hall. The servant opens the door, and Debbie always comes out and hovers timidly behind her. I know how frightened she must be of those servants, even after all these years. She gives me her big sad smile and says straight away, 'I've got lutkas on, Harryboy.'

Gus grunts, 'What you like, she cooks. When you come, I eat well.'

'Other times you starve?' I say. 'Where did you get that belly?'

'I'm down to my right weight,' he says. 'Ten years' time you should be as fat as me here.' He smacks his belly.

Debbie says, 'He plays squash two nights a week. It kills him.' She has a Benedictine. She always goes for sweet liqueurs.

So for supper we have potato lutkas, soup with meat balls and thin vermicelli, a half a chicken each with roast potatoes, sweet corn and cream spinach (the old folk, rest their souls, used to be Orthodox, but Gus and Debbie keep a modern home), and in case I'm hungry afterwards, Debbie brings out a big apple tart, with fruit salad and cream to finish. I ought to mention that we had a good white wine, at the right temperature. You think a bookmaker has to be a fat ignoramus? Gus knows all about wines, even if he hasn't got a butler. All the time, not a bad word.

After supper we are back in the lounge, and puffing our Havanas, and the storm breaks.

Gus looks at the ash on his cigar and starts quietly, as if he is delivering a stage soliloquy. 'A schlemiel I've got for a brother-in-law. A half-wit. A lunatic. A good wife I marry, and she has to have the village idiot for a brother. Can good ever come to a man without trouble?'

I keep dumb, breathe cigar smoke round myself. Now he addresses himself to me. 'Couldn't you do what I told you? Couldn't you leave well alone? For thirty years you been going to the tracks, don't you know when to call it a day? You were so greedy all of a sudden? You thought you were a genius? The prophet Elijah? You were getting your tips from the Almighty?'

Now he starts to lose his temper. He bangs his fist on his chest. 'From me you got the tip. Not the Almighty. Why should the Almighty care about *you*? A lowlife like you? Did you ever pay a subscription to a synagogue? At least I've got a seat, you should know what I pay for it. You? An atheist, I suppose. Go on, tell me you're an atheist.'

'I'm not an atheist.'

'A discussion now we're having about religion. Thank you. The intellectual. Thank you very much. Who's talking about religion? I'm talking about a tip. I tipped you a dog. It wasn't a gamble. What do I have to teach you at your time of life? It was a fix. The race was fixed. All you had to do was collect the money and go home. Go home, do you hear me? With the money in your pocket. My family, I do it for you because you're my family, my wife's brother, a tip like that I would never give to anyone, a fix you don't talk about. If they pulled my nails out...'

Does it matter what he said next? When the words are unwelcome, I can shut my ears up, curl up inside myself where it's nice and cosy, and dream. I dreamed.

When I come out of my trance, he is still going strong. 'A gambler. Too lazy to earn a living. My brother-in-law is a gambler. No, I'm sorry. A man of learning. I do you an injustice. I'm only a bookie. Illiterate. Race-cards I can read, that's all. All right, I can read a good novel as well as anyone. Go in the den, see my books. You should have the money I spend on books. They give it a big review on Sunday, I've got it on Monday. Every book they're talking about, you can see it when you go to Gus Van Bien's. Oh, I beg your pardon.' (He turns to poor Debbie, who has come in from the kitchen with the coffee trolley.) 'I do your brother an injustice. Your brother, the great reader. Did it do him any good, his reading? Did he learn a profession? On his back he lays all day, reading. At night he gambles. This is his profession.

'A man of forty-five. Have you got a wife? A home have you got? In Hackney he lives. In one stinking room. Hackney, he still lives there. Genius. A fine upstanding Jewish boy. My brother-in-law. A credit to me. Thank you.'

Then he starts to tell me how much he has done for me. Has he done his best or not? Fifty things he's tried for me. Fifty times he's had a straight talk with me. How many times has he given me money? All this is true. He is a good fellow, Gus, and I am a burden to him.

I had gone to ask for a loan, just a small one. You must understand from the start, although I am a cadger when necessary, you will never find me with the unshaven face, the dirty collar or frayed cuffs of a schnorrer. One thing about me, I always dress smartly. A good suit, midnight blue mohair, this year's cut. Dazzling white shirt, quiet tie of silk, rust-colour. Buy your clothes good if you have to starve afterwards.

I have to keep this front up. One evening I was walking through the West End with sixteen pounds in my pocket, my capital, all I had in the world. I met a couple I knew. 'How's things?' 'Fine, fine.' I heard myself— could I stop the words coming out?—telling them of a new deal I was in on. Property. Marvellous site. So what could I do next? I had them in a taxi, next thing we were sitting round a table at the White Tower. Come on, let's make an evening of it, my guests…Once I've started I have to go on. I urged them to try the smoked salmon. Would they like me to find out if there was any Beluga caviar? I was sick with fright. Sixteen pounds is only sixteen pounds. And to follow? Roast duck? Chicken barbecue? Steak Othello? And a good claret. And to follow? I was lucky. The bill only came to a little over twelve pounds. I threw three fives on the table and told the waiter to keep the change. I wasn't sick any more then. My guests had seen the bill. They had seen the tip. They saw how the waiters bowed me out. In the street I got a scare. What would they suggest next? More drinks? A night club? I tell you, I barely had taxi money. I gave them a big pitch about a showgirl I had to meet at eleven. Chuckles from male guest, 'Lucky fellow, you bachelors are the wise ones.' Big goodnights all round. Never seen them again. I tell you, I felt good. The next day I worried.

So now my pride swells up. I am a man at ease, with a cigar. 'Gus,' I say with quiet dignity, 'who is asking? Am I asking you for money? I come to my sister for dinner. Is there anything wrong with that?'

'Money,' says Gus. 'Who said you were asking for money? I gave you a tip—'

'Forget it, Gus. What's past is past. Never hold inquests on the past. A man in your position should know. Debbie has given us a wonderful dinner, God bless her. Can't we enjoy it? Can't you let me appreciate your cigar?'

'They cost seven-and-six each,' he says, 'wholesale. You want brandy with your coffee?'

In his rough way, Gus is a gentleman.

I got back to Hackney after midnight. I let myself into the house, trying to open the door quietly. Usually at this hour the whole house is dark. But tonight, from the back room on the ground floor I saw a light shining under the door. I heard voices and footsteps, which echoed the way they do in an empty room.

The downstairs flat had been vacant, but I knew from the old couple in the basement that a family was moving in soon. The old couple own the house. Their life savings are in it. They are always scrubbing stairs and landings as if they were polishing their jewels. For all their scrubbing, the house has the smell of all these tenement houses, a smell of cold decay that comes from the bare, aged lino that covers the floorboards in the hall and on the stairs.

I was warm with brandy. I wanted my bed and my dreams. I had no curiosity about the new tenants. In that back room were the people who were going to change my life, the new tenants sweeping their room out. But we never know what is coming to us.

I crept upstairs, as quietly as I could on the bare lino and the creaking floorboards, and I went to bed.

CHAPTER TWO

What Gus was doing his nut about was this. The day before he rang me in the afternoon, and gave me a cert for the third at Harringay.

Gus did this out of the goodness of his heart, because as he suggested to me after dinner, if you hear of such news and talk about it in his line of business, it is no good for trade. But Gus is always trying to put me on my feet.

The way he reckons is that if only I can get a little capital behind me, my normal human instincts will unfreeze, i.e., I will feel the need to start a nice secure little business. Then I will feel better, my sister Debbie will stop crying, Gus will mark a good deed up in heaven and incidentally will be shot of a parasite. Maybe a little shop, he suggests occasionally, a tobacconist and sweets. Or if I don't like work, I could buy an old house or two and let the rooms. Fine. To tell you the truth, this last proposition appeals to me a good deal. If the luck holds, I might live to old age. Did anyone ever hear of an old gambler?—a professional, I mean. Before then I must make some arrangement. So I dream of that thousand or two of capital, to buy a few houses for letting. And inside that dream, I snuggle up to the other dream, of going away to an island.

You may ask, why doesn't Gus put up the capital to start me in a business? He has. Several times. Every time I gambled it away. So now he's learned sense. Thank goodness for that. I wouldn't like my sister to be married to a fool. All the same, he tries to help.

In the evening I went to the track. I had some money with me, but as I was going in through the ten-shilling gate one of Gus's tuchas-lickers gave me an envelope. It had twenty pounds in it. Gus was even giving me the stake, bless him. I got five to one on my dog. Gus's twenty plus ten of my own brought me a hundred and fifty winnings.

So there it was, seventy minutes after I left home, my night's working profit, a hundred and fifty nicker. Now a professional, in gambling, is not greedy. Unless he has another sure thing, which is unlikely, he walks away from it. So I went up to the restaurant and had some supper.

But down there in front of me, through the high glass windows, the floodlights were on, the grass a bright unreal green, the dogs on parade; and I realised I was snapping my fingers for the best runner. I could have bet ten, twenty, put the rest away, but I was backing the favourite, and at eight to five where is the benefit if you are just going to bet with pocket-money? A hundred I put on, and when the dog strolled home, a hundred and sixty came back to me. So there it was, two hundred and ten nicker.

I let the fifth race go, did a combination on the sixth and won seventy. Two hundred and eighty nicker.

Now what happened next may be beyond my power to explain. It had happened before, and I suppose it will happen again. Sitting at my table on the terrace, I leaned back against the wooden wall that rose to form the front of the table above and behind me. I shut my eyes. A throbbing started in the middle of my chest. I opened my eyes and studied the card. The way my eyes bored into it you would have thought there was a computer clicking inside my head to give me the winner. But all I could hear inside my head was a buzz, a scrape on my nerves that keyed me up, wound me up to do the mad thing like a clockwork train. My eyes went up and down the names, but they only saw one name, the Number Five dog. I could give no reason. Simply, this was my dog.

I cannot tell what is in me at such times. There is something like death. Go on, go on, squeeze the trigger. Cold water pours into my lungs when I breathe. The muscles in my arms cramp. I am full of knots that are going to get tighter and tighter unless I put the money on. But there is also the exulting certainty that this is victory, this is the last skyline and Big Rock Candy Mountain is in front of me. Go on, Harryboy. Take a thousand pounds, two thousand pounds home with you. They'll be talking about you at the barber's shop tomorrow. All the schnorrers will be round you and you will hand out loans like an emperor. Harryboy Boas. Harryboy Boas, he walked away from Harringay with fifteen hundred nicker in his pocket.

But I know, I know what is going to happen. I pay in my money, all of it. There is no magic unless I pay in all of it. Keep back one pound and—but I can't. Who is making my fingers move? Not me. I lean back. I breathe deliberately. I become calm. The preparations, the race, the loudspeakers and the hubbub mean nothing to me. I know what is going to happen.

There he is, my dog, in orange. Loping down the track when the first, second and third have all shot home. I am calm, so calm, empty, drained empty. There is no regret in me, nothing, nothing. Only peace. I feel far away from it all. Now I can lay me down to sleep.

What the hell do they know?—the punters who come to the tracks or pop into the betting shops for a giggle? Or the professionals who keep it all on a debit and credit basis? None of them knows what a gambler is. The gambler is the one who goes on with no peace, no release, till he has annihilated himself. I am a gambler.

I was going down the steps when Gus came hurrying across, dripping happiness like gravy.

'Well, Harryboy? How you do?'

'Lend me a dollar for a taxi.'

After a few seconds, he says, 'I've finished with you.'

He is not a bad fellow. As you know, the next night he made me welcome for supper.

CHAPTER THREE

The Deaners moved into the house a week later. I didn't catch any glimpse of them before then. I am at the dog track most nights, and it fell out that our comings and goings didn't coincide, though I heard from the old man that they were giving the place a terrific spring-clean.

The day they moved in was a memorable one for me. Not because of them, for I couldn't know what they were to bring into my life, but because of a dog.

The night before, I had been to the track and brought off a hot forecast. This forecast was a funny business. I went to the tracks with two dogs tipped for the third race. When it came to the race, I saw a dog's name on the card. Heliotrope. I liked it. It wasn't one of the dogs they'd tipped, and the odds were diabolical. But I stood there, and I said the name to myself again and again, 'Heliotrope, Heliotrope.' It upset me. God knows what was buried in me, from childhood, for this name to upset me. I fancied the name. So I did it in the forecast. Now this is mad. It is stone bonkers meshuggah. This is the way women bet. So would you believe me, it came off? I walked away from the track with a hundred and ten quid in my pocket. I knew what might happen if I stayed for the last three races. None of that nonsense. I walked away from the track with a hundred and ten quid in my pocket and a light heart.

The next morning I was in the West End, in a winner's mood, panting to play the millionaire and buy myself something snazzy. Well, this time it wasn't a suit or a half-a-dozen shirts. It was a set of the works of Emile Zola translated into English. I saw the books in Charing Cross Road—once I get to that row of bookshops you can say goodbye to me for half a day—and the next thing I knew I owned this stack of two dozen fat books and I was shouting for a taxi to get them home. This Zola is a terrific writer. He can be tougher than Mickey Spillane, and when he gets on to sex he's red hot. But I am giving you the wrong idea about him. He is a serious writer. Profound. Terrific.

I knew what my programme was going to be for the next few weeks. I can go off on a jag with books like some people do with liquor. Weeks at a time. When I get on to a good writer I have to go right through him. So now, for the next couple of months, I looked forward to doing nothing at all. Nothing, except laying on my bed (just like Gus said) and reading through this stack of books. I would stay with them as long as my money lasted.

My room was at the top of the house, quiet. The street is half a slum, but in front of the house and in the garden behind it, are trees that no one has tended for years. This was in the winter. All I could see from my room was sky, and bare tree-tops. For weeks I could lie on my bed and read. A hundred and ten quid would see me through. What did I want except rent and meal money? I was always a great reader. When I was a boy I even dreamed of writing books.

So I settled down—(You lovely dog, Heliotrope. What buried memory in me did you touch? What buried memory in the owner's mind made him give you the name? Here was I, free for weeks, I could dream, I could weep, I could follow the long, long trail of my thoughts, because a dog was named Heliotrope. This is how our fortunes, life or death, are decided)—I settled down on my bed and read all the morning. All of a sudden I heard the factory whistle from the next street. Half-past twelve. Pavlov's dog felt hungry. I went downstairs. When I opened the front door, a big furniture van blotted out the view. As far as I could see it was deserted. Naturally. The British working-man had heard the lunch whistle and bolted. Half a mile to the caff in five seconds flat. Oh, I could make some money racing *them* against greyhounds.

There are two places I go to for meals. The Italian café near the corner, and the kosher restaurant down the road. Today I felt good. Reading is wonderful, but reading on a full belly is the peak of human happiness. I had roast breast of veal, a strudel and a glass of lemon tea, and walked around for a half-hour to clear my head before the afternoon session.

Fellows ask me, especially when my wallet is full, why I should live in Hackney. Why not?—that's enough to answer.

Still, there is more to it. A lot of gambling fellows live in the West End, near the whores and the restaurants. Me? I want to live where I grew up. God knows, there's no one left—hardly anyone, a face here and there—but that's why the place holds me. There's only the place left.

Also, I like it. Here it is, a Victorian-Edwardian suburb swallowed up by London, broad streets, little villas and big tradesmen's houses; and now, among these, factories and workshops everywhere, little workshops in the mews, big yellow-brick factories on the corner sites. Traffic roars in the streets. Here, all sorts live. The Cockneys are of the old breed, sharp-faced, with the stamp of the markets on them. The young Jews either look like pop singers or pop singers' managers. The old ones—it's funny, the pious old men with yellow beards I remember from my childhood seem to have died off, all of them, but the old women survive. Among the crowds you can see the old women, women you might have seen in the East End fifty years ago (Hackney isn't the East End—that's the mark of the outsider, when you hear someone call Hackney the East End. The East End starts two miles down the road, across the border of Bethnal Green) schlapping their big shopping bags.

Ingram's Terrace—this is where I roomed—is part of a street that joins Stoke Newington High Street next to Amhurst Road, not far north of Dalston Junction. It was probably named after the Victorian spec builder who ran it up; mostly two-storied houses, with basements; some bigger like old-fashioned vicarages; and the end houses with passages at the sides from street to back garden. Big rooms, high ceilings with mouldings on them; small areas in front that used to have hedges or fancy iron railings but since the war have wooden fences or nothing at all; neglected gardens at the back trampled and heaped with rubbish. When I was a boy, these houses were occupied by superior working-class families, who kept them in beautiful condition. Every year, when the fresh gravel and tar was laid on the road (I can still smell the tar) the houses were bright with fresh paint. Now most of them are tenements. The street is still clean. All the people are in work. Their cars jam the kerbs on both sides. All is quiet and decent. Negroes have come to live, more every month. And Cypriots. The Negroes are of marvellous respectability. Every Sunday morning they all go to the Baptist Chapel in the High Street. You should see the men, in beautiful pearl-grey suits and old-fashioned trilbies with curled brims, the big women full of dignity, and the little girls in white muslin and bonnets. It slays me. They are the Victorian residents of this street, come back a century later, with black skins. And the Cypriots—they gather at their gates, throwing their children in the air and kissing them when they come down.

The people in Ingram's Terrace don't mix, but they all say 'good morning' to each other. I never smelt any hatred between one kind and another, not even an ember that might flare up in the future. Of course, they all have good jobs. The children mix. The children all play in the street together. I love to watch them. The children are the only real common ground of the grown-ups. The Yiddisher mumma who comes out with a cake for her boy will bring cakes for the kids he's playing with, black, Cypriot, Gentile, the lot. Cockney women will gather round a pram to squeal, 'Ooh, isn't she pretty?' over a Negro baby. And vice versa.

So I had my half-hour walk round the houses, enjoying all this and some fresh sunshine for good measure. When I went back to the house the furniture men were unloading the van. The first thing I noticed was what they were carrying. It was cheap-contemporary. You know the sort of thing. Bright colours, uncomfortable designs, thin wood you could put your foot through. In the Terrace, taste still runs to solid furniture. ('At least let it *look* like it's worth the money.') Well, young people. The old man told me the new people were a young couple with a baby. Gentiles.

A girl was standing in the hall, telling the removal men where to put things. This must be the wife. Not my type at all. Thin, lank hair, jumper and skirt. What I call the Olive Oyl type. Next to her was a kid. A little boy, about four. A proper little bruiser. 'This is the baby?' I thought. 'That little tearaway's gonna make trouble in the house. A quiet house. Goodbye to my quiet house.' At the moment, the kid wasn't making a sound. He was watching the operation in the dumbstruck, hypnotised way kids sometimes have, absolutely still, big eyes taking everything in, standing very close to his mama, hand on her skirt.

Siskin, the landlord, stood at the top of the basement stairs. He lives in the basement with his wife. I wouldn't put a dog in that basement, and I hate dogs. They live in the basement, and the rest of the house is their income. Siskin is a small grey man who looks like a mouse, and he lives like one. He hardly ever comes up out of his hole. When he does, he puts his head timidly round the door from the basement stairs. You'd think he was making sure that it was all clear. Then he comes into the hall, and the way he watches you, you're afraid to speak too loud in case he bolts back down his hole.

Siskin said nothing. I said 'Afternoon,' to the girl. She gave me a cautious, new-neighbour smile and said, 'Good afternoon,' and I went upstairs.

It wasn't so easy to concentrate in the afternoon. I could hear the bumpings and scrapings of furniture down below, and the voices of the removal men.

Once or twice I heard the kid's voice. I couldn't make out the words. Just a yell of protest or a whine of appeal. A kid. Such was my luck. Well, on a full belly, the next best thing to reading is a good sleep, so I got under the blankets.

The sunlight had gone out of the room when I woke up. I felt muzzy, and I tried to focus on the noise that had woken me up. I couldn't hear anything. Then I heard it again, a soft thump. I got out of bed and sluiced some cold water over my face. I dried myself, and listened. Silence again. Then the thump. Then silence. Then the thump.

It sounded like the cupboard on the landing. But Miss Gosling wasn't in yet. Miss G. was an ancient spinster who served in a draper's down Kingsland Road. She'd worked there about fifty years. The shop is a survival from the past, the sort of place you read about in *Kipps*. It keeps going because you can get good bed linen there at low prices. Miss Gosling was also what you might call a survival. Her older sister, who had shared the room with her and worked at the same shop, had died the year before. The older one, Miss Maud, used to be a real old darling, but the one that was left, Miss Ethel, was the sour type, and since she was on her own she'd got worse. Her bedsitter was on the landing facing my room but three steps down, and her gas stove was out on the landing. Since her sister's death she never seemed to use it. As far as I could tell she lived almost entirely on those sticky sweets with pretty wrappers we used to call Russian bonbons. She had them weighed out from the jar in the shop round the corner, and she threw the used wrappers all over the landing. In her sister's time the pair of them used to keep themselves and the place spick and span. I didn't see much of the old woman shut up in her room, but my opinion was that she must be going dotty in there. Anyway, the cupboard, although it was up on my landing, was hers.

There's no cat in the house. The moving van had driven away, or I'd have assumed one of the blokes had come prowling up to see what he could knock off.

I looked out of my door. There was no one on the landing. There was no draught to shake the cupboard door. I went back to my room. I waited inside the door. Then I heard the floorboards on the landing creak. I opened my door again quickly. The cupboard door was open, and the kid was coming out of the cupboard. He just stood there and looked at me.

I said, 'You havin' a look in the cupboard, kid?'

He didn't say anything. I said, 'There's only old cases in there. It's dusty. Your mum won't like it.'

He didn't answer. I said, 'Show us your hands.' He didn't move, so I leaned down, carefully so as not to frighten him, and looked at his hands. They were covered with dirt.

'I don't mind you comin' up,' I said, 'but this cupboard isn't mine. It belongs to a lady. She doesn't like me to open it, so I don't reckon you ought to, unless she says you can.'

I asked him his name. He stood there with his lips clamped.

Then his mother called up from the hall. 'Gregory.'

'I know your name. It's Gregory,' I said. 'My name is Harryboy.'

She called him again, this time a kind of sharp, annoyed yelp. 'Gregory. Where are you? Come down at once.'

He gave me a look as if everything I'd said had been a tough trial of his patience, and kept his lips pressed together like a little magistrate. I didn't know if it was me he was fed up with or his mum. He turned round and started to trot downstairs.

His mum was up on the landing already by the time he'd got down the first flight. The landing is where the bathroom and lavatory are. We all use them. 'Gregory,' she said, 'I told you not to wander all over the house.' She looked up at me. 'Has he been annoying you? I'm ever so sorry.'

'It's all right,' I said. 'You can't shut kids up.'

She said, 'He's got to learn to behave himself. You won't be troubled, Mr—?'

'Boas.'

'Pleased to meet you. Our name is Deaner.' She said all this without any good nature. I know these women. They don't sound nasty, just nervy and abrupt all the time. The kid stood next to her. He was all docile, all of a sudden. He was small but very sturdy in his build, with the sort of short chubby kids' legs that get you. When he was on the landing with me, he faced me as if I was a big dog he mustn't be frightened of. But now, next to his mum, he wasn't frightened, just lifeless. She was going on. 'He generally behaves himself. It's just over-excitement, all the new surroundings.'

I said, 'Sure. You fixed up all right? Anything I can help?'

Her kind of woman is very funny. She went from being just nervy to—well, she just hardened as she stood there, and her face clenched. Anyone'd think I'd asked her up to my bedroom. She said, and it was plain hostile, 'My husband will see to everything when he gets home. Come on.' This was to the kid. She looked up from the bottom of the stairs. 'I'll see he doesn't bother you.'

I said, 'That's all right.' I went back to my room.

I looked at my Zola books. I reckoned the kid was too small to be at school. That's all I wanted, a kid stamping up and down the stairs. Fat chance I had of reading in peace.

Hi-aye, big sigh. Not time for supper yet. I got back into bed and pulled the blankets over me. I can sleep all day and night if I want to.

CHAPTER FOUR

From too much staying in bed I got the jack up to my eyebrows, so I went to see Marcia. Marcia is the only lady I ever knew. She lives in Half Moon Street near Piccadilly and she charges twenty pounds for a short time. I can only enjoy the best.

She is at least thirty-five, but she has a skin like a young girl and what she's got she uses better than any girl. She is tall and elegant, but solid in the flesh and muscular. An athlete. Splendid breasts. She was married to a bank manager once. They had a good car and a house in one of those expensive Buckinghamshire villages. The life bored her and by the time she'd got through all the men in the neighbourhood she started to ask herself, why should she let them have it for nothing? So she went into business. Why not? If I was a woman, I'd sell it.

She isn't the sort that tells her pathetic story to the customers, but after I'd seen her a few times I took her out one night to the dogs and won more for her than she would have earned staying at home. She stood me a supper and told me about herself. She chats to you like a man, relaxed and independent, her eyes casing you all the time. She aims to retire when she's forty. In the meantime she's buying houses and letting rooms. It must have been from her as well as Gus that I got the idea of doing the same thing some day. She is already a woman of means. Also the classiest tramp in the West End of London.

I rang up and the maid answered, but Marcia took the phone away from her. 'Harryboy,' she said. 'How nice. Give me an hour to get rid of this one and we'll make a night of it.' She does that sometimes. No extra charge. If she likes you.

Some men don't go much for whores. They need a woman to cling round their necks saying she loves them. I have to admit that I only feel relaxed with a whore. With the others, you never know what they are after. I am a free man. All my life I have gone my way, and no one has managed to take possession of my life or make me responsible for theirs. It nearly happened once, with a Frenchwoman. We lived together for a few months. For me, it was just an arrangement. I liked the girl, but only as good company for a while. For a while, that was the point. I liked her enough to look after her and give her all the good breaks I could. But not for life. I didn't mean it to be for life. But I came to see that she was thinking of it that way. They all do, all the so-called normal women do. It's biology. So I left her.

Marcia and I had a real old rough and tumble that night. We always did. You can only enjoy Marcia if you accept that she is not one of these courtesan types you read about who minister to the male with all the ancient arts of womanhood and all that jazz. She is tough. She despises men. They are just implements to her, and even when they are paying her she just uses them. The secret with her is for the man, on his side, to use her. Not to give way to her, like most of her clients apparently do, but to bash for his own satisfaction and no consideration for her. I'm no sadist. I don't mean that. I mean just self-interest.

This is the only way. The man should look after his interests and the woman after hers. I detest a woman if she clings to me. In the back of my head I start to wonder what she wants from me. If she's tough and independent and out for herself, I feel safe. I can like her genuinely then. Hence the whores.

Debbie, my darling sister, has been begging me for twenty years to get married. Can I explain all this to her? Not only the intimate things. Debbie and I have never talked about such matters. But about freedom—could I make her understand what freedom means? I never told her about the Frenchwoman even, and this is an important part of my story, as you will understand when I tell you.

In between, Marcia brought sandwiches and whisky from the kitchen. We drank most of a bottle. We can both take liquor. I like the warm jolt that comes with each shot. It means no more to me than that. I can do without it. The worst disgrace that could fall on me is to be drunk, even mildly. It hasn't happened yet. Marcia talked to me about property. She said the surest bet these days was to buy stuff in the East End. 'My God, Harry,' she said, 'you can buy whole streets. The owners practically go down on their knees to sell. What are you waiting for? You have a look round Saint George's and Whitechapel. Slums. You buy them for the last five years before clearance and stuff them with niggers. They'll pay the earth for a room. You could clean up, Harry. You don't need much capital, you can buy a house for two hundred.'

I said, 'Whores are supposed to have hearts of gold. Lend me.'

'Not this whore.'

We slept healthy and I went home with the milk, through needling February rain. This was how I got to say good morning to Miss Gosling, who I hardly ever saw these days.

I got in before eight. From the kitchen on the ground floor I could hear the little boy wailing. As I went upstairs the smell of burning milk got stronger. Miss Gosling was on the top landing, staring down over the banisters like a character in a horror film. On her gas stove in the corner, a pan of milk was boiling over.

I pointed this out to her. She didn't seem to hear. She just peered at me. She had unhappy, protruding eyes with big pouches under them. She was one of those tall, old-fashioned ladies who would be stately if they stood upright but they have a grim kind of stoop with the shoulders hunched in. Her black dress came down to the tops of her shoes like in old-fashioned photos. It used to be shining in her sister's time but now it was dull and blotchy with stains.

I said again, 'Good morning, Miss Gosling. Your milk's caught.' She didn't move, so I turned the gas off. She said, 'It's been going on since six o'clock.'

I said, 'A kid in the house, what do you expect?'

'It's going to be like this every day,' she said. 'I know it. My nerves won't stand it.'

'We have to make way for the young,' I said.

'What about my nerves, Mr Boas? I've suffered from my nerves ever since I was a child.'

The yells were coming non-stop, high and piercing. I said, 'Too bad.'

'This used to be such a nice quiet house,' she said. 'I knew he was a nasty little boy. He was in the sweet shop. He came and stood near me when I was buying my sweets and he looked at me. He wanted to beg. I could see it. He would have begged from me if his mother hadn't been there. I hate children who beg. In my childhood a little boy who begged would have been whipped. Children were properly brought up in my day.'

I managed to close my door on her. I changed into slippers and a fresh shirt. Then, as it was a Friday, I went down to give the old man his rent.

He worries. If I don't go down he is liable to creep upstairs and disturb my morning sleep.

Gregory's parents were trying to hush him up when I went past. But he was yelling back at them and Miss Gosling and the whole world.

Siskin was in his cellar drinking lemon tea. I think he sleeps in his shirt, on which I've never seen a collar, and his face is always hairy like a gooseberry.

He looks up at me. His wrinkled old woman pauses with an armful of dirty sheets, squints her bitter stare at me and shuffles into the back room.

He starts, 'You been out with a woman.' (What it sounds like is 'You bin aht mid àh vooman' like a corny character actor, but this I will leave to corny character actors.)

I put his thirty-five shillings on the table. 'Make me a cup of tea.'

He counts the money. Every week he counts it, not suspiciously but trembling as if when it is spent he will starve. 'From a woman you can get germs.'

'For twenty nicker you don't get germs.'

'They cost more?' Now he is pouring me a cup of tea. It comes bitter and brown out of the big iron pot. Like the tea of my childhood. He lives on his old age pension and on the three pounds or so a week he makes on rents from this house after expenses. His four children have all inherited his lifetime's ill luck. The two girls married washouts. The two boys got sick wives. All four men are the kind of schlemiels who sweep out workshop floors. The worst thing that ever happened to old Siskin was when the four children agreed to pay five shillings each towards his keep. The quarrels about who paid and who did not pay broke up the family. All the children stopped paying on the grounds that the rest weren't paying, and most of the time they are so ashamed that they keep away from their parents.

He jerks his thumb at the ceiling. 'You hear?'

'At least some life in the house.'

'Forty-five shillings a week, thank God. I would be in my box before my own children helped.'

'Who is he?' I jerked my thumb up.

'The father? A bookkeeper. You know the supermarket on the corner in Dalston? There he keeps books. A decent feller.'

'Gregory,' I said. 'What a name. You can know people by the names they inflict on their kids.'

I went upstairs. The kid was still howling. He was getting hoarse and desperate and heartbroken but he was as loud as ever as he passed the two-hour mark. By their voices, the parents were tiring fast. In bed I listened. A childhood is one long rearguard action of naked free will against society. Every fit of howling is a Famous Last Stand, an Alamo, a Thermopylae, a heroic little tragedy. This fine thought must have made music of the noise, because I fell asleep.

I woke up and reached for my watch. It was three in the afternoon. I was dressing myself to go out for a sandwich, not an attractive idea on a dark, wet February afternoon but a necessity of the belly, when I heard scuffling in the hall cupboard again.

I opened my door as quietly as I could and went out in my socks. The cupboard door was slightly ajar. I opened it slowly. The little boy was curled up at the bottom. He lay on his side with his knees drawn up and his hands against his chest, the fingers of each hooked like claws. There was no trace of the morning's tears in his face. It was the mask of childhood, an utter clarity that no one could penetrate. We looked at each other.

I said, 'Lion?'

'Tiger.'

I stepped back into my room and came back with a saucer of milk, which I put on the floor. 'Tigers like milk.'

'You be a daddy tiger.'

'What do I do?'

He came out of the cupboard, pointing to the saucer. 'Lick it up.'

The clear eyes looked at me out of that little mask, waiting to repel the next grown-up assault. His mother's voice shrilled, 'Gregory!' A second later, from an open doorway, 'Gregory!'

He looked at me and shrugged, like a long-suffering old man, and began to jump down the stairs with his feet together. From the landing below he shouted, 'How old am I?'

'Four?'

With indignation: 'Nearly five. I can jump three stairs.'

A female yell: 'Gregory!' I heard the thud of his last jump, and the protesting squeal of his voice as his mother dragged him into their flat and slammed the door.

Going back to my room, I saw that he had left one of his miniature cars in the cupboard.

I knocked at their door at half-past seven. As I had thought, supper was over, for behind the noise of someone getting up to open the door, I could hear guns blazing and the Marshal of Dodge City shouting, 'Throw your guns out, Ringo, you haven't got a chance.'

A fellow opened the door, about thirty, fair-haired. 'Yes?'

The TV set was in the far corner. Gregory sat in front of it, hands between his knees. He glanced round at me. He didn't know me. Absolute blank in the eyes. He turned back to the gunfight. The table in the middle of the room had big sheets of ruled paper spread out on it and open books propped on other books. Dad, at the door, had a pencil in his hand. He must have been doing his homework to a background of Dodge City. God Bless Our Happy Home.

I held out the toy. 'Your little boy dropped this.'

'Thanks. Gregory—' The kid did not hear. Just that awful stillness in front of the set, hands pressed between his knees, and that awful drinking-in stare at the screen. 'Gregory, thank the gentleman.'

From the kitchen door, 'Gregory!' Mum was washing up.

I said, 'That's all right. He's enjoying himself. I reckon I'm keeping you from your work.'

'Don't worry about that. Come in.' He turned round. 'Evelyn—'

Prompted, she did her duty. 'I'll pour you a cup of tea, Mr—?'

'Boas.' God forbid a housewife should fail to offer a cup of tea, even to her worst enemy. The husband asked me to sit down and I did. I am not neighbourly. I have no friends, and I don't try to make them. But I get interested.

I nodded at the papers on the table. 'You work overtime?'

'My exams. I'm taking my exams next year. There's a lot to do.'

The wife set my tea down in front of me. 'My husband is going to be a company secretary. It generally takes three years and he's going to do it in two. It's all in his spare time.' This was her programme, you felt from the ring in her voice, not his. He sat dumb, playing with the pencil. She said, 'If he passes, his boss is going to find an opening for him. Of course, his prospects are wonderful. You can end up secretary of a really important company. And then of course there's the Stock Exchange tips. That's where the money is these days. You can make a fortune.'

To bring him in I said to him, 'How you finding it here?'

She answered, 'It isn't what we were looking for, Mr Boas, but you have to take what you can find these days.' She was cold and upright. If she did all the talking, it was not in friendliness, but because it was her duty to speak proudly for her family to all comers. 'Still,' she said, 'we shan't be here for long.'

The husband said, 'It isn't so bad really. It's this one I'm worried about.' He indicated the kid. 'This damn' rain. It keeps him in all day. No wonder he's fidgety. He ought to be in the park.'

'I take him out.' She addressed this to the husband. It sounded like continued-from-our-last. 'I take him out every time I go shopping. How can I take him in the park in this weather? You don't want him to get pneumonia. I took him out three times today. He runs away from me in the market. I keep telling him, and he runs away and laughs at me.'

'All right, Evelyn.'

'He could have an accident. Those lorries. I'm terrified all the time. He doesn't care. He just laughs when I tell him.' She turned to me, as if I was responsible. 'This isn't a very nice environment for a child.'

'Where have you moved from?'

'We had a flat in Ilford. Only they put the rent up. Mummy and Daddy live in Ilford. They have a nice house, but of course they haven't got room for us.' I could have told you all about Evelyn before she spoke. A suburban. Our street must be like the bottom of a dustbin to her. I could have told you from this flat. In the front bedroom (I had seen before the curtains went up) a full bedroom suite. In this room, a three-piece lounge suite plus dining-room table and sideboard. Not to mention the telly. An Evelyn must have all this even if she's living in a cupboard. It's her wedding ring. She will pay for it on the never-never and feed her family on rabbit food. The furniture is her ultimatum to the husband. He was to work like some foredoomed male insect till he can get the house all this is meant for. She continued the apology. 'We came here to be near Vic's mother. She's ailing.'

Vic's voice of apology was for her. 'She's all on her own.'

'Of course,' Evelyn said, 'we shall put money down for a house as soon as Vic is established.'

'He'll be all right—' I was talking about the kid.

He sat with his back to us, a little wood carving. 'Wait till he gets out in the street. He wants other kids to play with.'

'I shouldn't like him to play with the ones I've seen,' she said. 'I do hope we shall find him a suitable playmate. And a suitable school.' Then she launched her counter-attack. 'What do you do, Mr Boas?'

'Me? I'm in property.' What else could I say?

'Really?' Her eyes called me liar. In property, and living up in that attic? 'I hear it's a very paying business.'

Back up, Boas, you're in the crap. 'It will be. The great thing is not to get big-headed. You know, buy a house, buy a car. You know the way some people are.' Oh, Boas, that tongue of yours! Cut it out, someone cut it out! 'Me, I take it steady. I got houses, you know. In the East End I got houses. You can pick 'em up dead cheap these days. Round Whitechapel, Saint George's. There's a fortune in it. Only you see, I take it steady. I live here. Economise. All my money goes into the houses. I don't like mortgages, liabilities. Put all the money back in the business, that's my motto. Live simple for a few more years.'

'Very wise.' The programme had finished. She turned to the kid. 'Switch it off, Gregory.'

'Only another half-hour, Mummy.'

A whip-crack. 'Switch it off! Or I'll never let you stay up again.'

He switched off and got up. He had his mother's dark hair and eyes, but a sturdiness that came from neither parent. He said to me, 'Can I see your houses?'

With his back to us, away in his own world, he had heard. They hear and see everything. His mother said, 'That's enough, Gregory. Go out and clean your teeth.'

'Can I?'

'Gregory!'

I winked a 'yes' at him as he went out to the kitchen.

I should have gone then, but the disbelief in her eyes had upset me. Disbelief of my lies always makes me desperate. I heard myself saying, 'Well, now we're neighbours, perhaps you'll let me take you out one night. To supper.'

She said, 'You mustn't bother, Mr Boas.'

'No bother. We'll go up West. I may be economical here, you know, but up West I live. We'll go somewhere smart, shall we? Does she like champagne, Mr Deaner?'

You should have seen the hope in his face. It was bright like a child's. Not for the champagne, but for the friendship. This was a lonely man. 'Call me Vic. Champagne, well, I don't know.'

'Mr Boas—'

'Champagne, smoked salmon, the lot. Don't worry about the money. It's all on the expense account. That's the best of being in business. You ask your husband. He knows all about expense accounts. Eh, Vic?'

'We'll talk about it another time, Mr Boas—'

Vic started, 'I'll go out for some beer—'

'Vic, you really must get on with your work. Mr Boas, I have to put Gregory to bed.'

'Sure, sure…' I made for the door. 'It's a date, Vic, eh?'

'Sure.'

So I was stuck with it. My big mouth.

CHAPTER FIVE

I couldn't settle down to my reading the next morning. All this talk about owning property had unsettled me. After all, Marcia had said there was a fortune in it. The houses were waiting to be picked up. So I went down to the East End to look for some property. Why not?

I got off the bus at Leman Street and walked down into Cable Street. The wind was cold off the river, lashing rain into my face, and carrying the wheep-wheep of ships' sirens. I used to love that noise when I was a kid. I could hear it from my bed, six blocks away, where we lived till we moved to Hackney. I used to hang round the warehouse backs in Wapping, sniffing that close spicy smell, and our favourite playground was among the cannon on the Tower promenade. There was a whole gang of us. Debbie was one of us. You wouldn't believe it, this suburban matron in her smart dresses, with her three smart daughters, she ran with a gang of rough boys in these cobbled streets, she ruled those boys, she ruled me, she protected me, and I worshipped my heroic big sister.

Debbie, fat Debbie, so gentle and bewildered in your mink coat, I have seen you swinging from the tailboard of a brewer's wagon as it thundered over those cobbles, the carter in his leather apron turning on his perch and lashing at you with his whip, while we ragamuffin boys ran alongside hooting him, cheering you and pelting his two great horses with lumps of coal. Do you remember, Debbie? Does it seem far away, another life? Does it prick your eyes with tears?

Property? As soon as I had stepped into this street, the dream of money was gone. The other dream had taken its place. I cannot come to the East End without leaving present times behind me and entering the world of the past. And the pain is this, that my too, too solid flesh in the world of the past is like a ghost of the past in the solid world of the present; it can look on but it cannot touch.

I walked down Cable Street—this once respectable street of working people that is now a garbage heap of lost, ferocious schwartzers and the wretchedest of whores—and I stopped at a gap in the decaying shops, and I cried. In the rain I stood and cried. This bomb crater, patches of diseased weeds, black puddles, rusty bedsteads, sodden newspapers, old prams, smashed packing-cases and the turds of tramps—this is where my mother died.

It was her luck, the last months of the war, she came to help a widowed friend get the tea and sandwiches ready for when the men got back from the funeral, and a flying-bomb dropped on the house. My mother, my golden mother, she and my father the lord and lady of my golden childhood, this is where she vanished out of life. I came home from the army and my mother did not exist any more. Not even a body. Not even a gravestone.

I walked away from the pain, but it was waiting for me in Hessel Street where she used to shop, the last ghetto market, a clutter of stalls and holes in the wall smelling of poultry and vegetables and groceries. And in the tenement of dark red brick on the other side of Commercial Road where we lived, I stood in the entry and filled myself with the smells—it is always the smells that work on me—a thickness of mixed cooking, laundry on the boil and the odours of many people close together. I love it, the stink of home, of all that is good.

My father would be seventy-five if he was alive now. But he died two years ago in the London Hospital. He had an illness, it was like rotting away, they cut one leg off at the knee, then the other, then one from the thigh, then the other. He lay there and joked, mild and affectionate, the papa of our childhood. But at the end there was no affection in his eyes. He just had the strength to lift the lids from eyes glazed in bitterness, and close them again, and turn his head away from us, as if to say, 'Who are these strangers? Who do they think they are fooling, squeezing my hand and murmuring to me? Why don't they leave me alone?' There were tubes in him and his breath snored. I grasped Debbie's arm and pushed her away, and we left him alone to die. This is how it ends. This and in a crater full of garbage. In Fieldgate Street round the corner I found the little synagogue he used to go to. It had been bombed and rebuilt. I was bar-mitzvahed here. I used to come here with him for the Festivals, proud to go with him when I was small, holding his hand and seeing how everybody greeted him. He was a religious man. Like my mother he was full of real charity, which means goodness and a cheerful heart. He was everybody's friend. Was God his friend, when he died?

As I was coming out into Whitechapel Road I caught up with an old fellow carrying a mountain of boxes. The rain was teeming down. This was one of those old Yiddles who are stooped but thickset with muscle, faces of iron, keen blue eyes; ageless proletarians. Eighty years old, maybe, and still humping boxes in the rain. I took some of them and saw him across to Black Lion Yard. There came no thanks. The only words he spoke to me were, in a tone of strong grievance, 'Hot nisht an umbrelly?'

Marvellous. He made me cheerful again. In Black Lion Yard I couldn't resist stopping at the old dairy. There used to be a cow-house here in my childhood. Mother used to bring me for a treat to buy warm milk from the cows. I can remember them, big, sad patient creatures, Debbies all of them, in their dark byres. Years after they were gone, you could still go into the yard and smell the rotten straw, and it was like being a child again. But now the wooden gates, ten-foot high, were closed. I stuck my nose through a crack and sniffed, but no smell of the past lingered. And as I came away I saw on a board that epitaph to all our yesterdays, 'Acquired for development by—'

So a salt beef sandwich in Bloom's. On white, with fat and plenty of mustard.

Leaning up against the counter in Bloom's was a character I knew from the tracks, and he said he was going over to the Club. Like a schmock I went with him. This club is in an alley off Aldgate. Not just a spieler but a right dive. The worst gang in London used to hang out there till they moved up West. The police leave it open because if they want a word with some East End villain it's odds on they'll find him there.

In this place they play eleven-to-four rummy. Show me a way of losing money and I will try it. I went in there with eighty pounds in my wallet and I came out skint. The man who was going to buy property. Such is my form.

This happy day led to my getting a job.

CHAPTER SIX

Yes, from time to time I work. There are occasions when the defeat of going into a factory is less than the defeat of going to Gus for another loan. I have a trade. A Hoffmann presser.

I went into the tailoring when I was fifteen. My father, God rest his soul, was a cigarette-maker. He had a weak chest and he worked at home. He was at his table day and night. For what they paid him he had to work day and night. Coughing. Me he wanted to be a scholar. The Almighty only knows what dreams my father had for me. Only now when he is dead do I feel sorrow for the disappointment I must have caused him, which he never showed. Never did he have a reproach for me. I won a scholarship when I was ten. I was a clever kid. A good Hebrew scholar, too. So I went to a high school. The family intellectual. They used to read my essays out to the other boys. Ten out of ten for composition. The kicks I got from putting words on paper! And books, I gobbled books like peanuts. How I didn't wear my eyes away I don't know. But a lowlife is a lowlife. I was losing money on the cards at fourteen, and going with my pals to shilling whores. Money I needed, for cigarettes and women and pride in my pocket. I left school when I was fifteen and got a job in the tailoring.

Well, after I'd done my last winnings I went into this workshop. It was a good place. I took home sixteen pound a week. I was there six weeks. All this time I was a good boy. I wanted to get a wad of stake money together for the flat racing season. At the barber's shop, where normally I lose as much money as I do at the tracks, I only stayed long enough to get my haircut, hot towel and shampoo. I stayed home at nights reading Zola. I played solo with the fellows at work in lunch-breaks, but this was for pennies. To lose five shillings was a catastrophe in that place. The Deaners I only saw in glimpses. To be honest, I kept out of their way. This working-man phase was embarrassing to me.

The time passed pleasantly. The fellows in the shop were a good lot. Wisecracks and practical joking go on all the time. It's warm. I like the machine roar from the big shops and the bray of music while you work. This factory was also very convenient for women. You took them down to the basement in the goods lift and shagged them on the bales. It was always the way I like it, no more than lighting your cigarette from a stranger's. These factory girls are peasants. It's a kind of sex war all the time. There's this tribe of girls at their machines. Each time you go past, to the lav or the foreman's cubicle, you can feel them sizing you up as if you are a bull in the auction ring, and sometimes they give you a razzing. One of them took my fancy, a real hard brazen bit. She never let me pass without a dirty crack. One lunch-break when the bell rang I went across to her and said, 'I fancy you.'

She said, 'Do you? Come back when you've grown one.'

I said, 'I'll knock the back out of you, Susie.'

She said, 'It's got teeth in, mate.'

I said to her, 'Come on. I'm playing cards in ten minutes.'

When we'd come upstairs again I could hear her reporting back to the girls and them shrieking with laughter. We never took any more notice of each other after that except that I got a bit more razzing.

In the meantime the flat racing season started. I opened an account with a telephone bookie named Ockley, in the High Street. It just took my fancy to open this account. It might give me more freedom of action, and lifting up the phone to make a casual bet was the kind of gesture I liked. I was in work when I fixed it up, with some money in the bank and a respectable sister with a Finchley address, so with him I was kosher. The first day at Lincoln I copped a winner and my balance in hand jumped back to two hundred.

I was a gentleman of leisure again. I packed in my job and spent my first sweet day of freedom in bed.

*　　　　*　　　　*

In the front bay window of the house, which was the Deaners' bedroom window, fancy net curtains went up. They had that bluey, misty look, and they were flounced and draped in a real high society way. In Ingram's Terrace, where most of the front curtains look like old bedcovers, this was as startling as the Stars and Stripes over the Kremlin. And it was, of course, just that—Evelyn Deaner's banner of defiance. She might not be here for long—I was to hear this statement from her frequently—but she meant to make the best of it.

I was in no hurry to see more of the Deaners. My invitation to them was one of those crazy traps I am always laying for myself, and I didn't want to fall into it. But I had plenty of evidence of their presence. From my room I could hear Evelyn Deaner on the go all day long. The hall was clean enough, but she sprayed it with some sweet-smelling disinfectant that took my appetite away every time I went out for a meal. She hung a roll of pink toilet paper in the lavatory, her contribution to gracious living. In the bathroom she put up a quite unnecessary notice, 'Kindly clean out bath after use.—E.D.'

She was a worker, that one. All day long I heard her on the go. She was so frail and sallow, I wondered where she got the energy from. I wondered how she could find so much to do in a two-room flat. But both questions are pointless when applied to these crazy-houseproud women. They cannot rest. They scurry about their domains as tirelessly and mindlessly as some breed of toiling insect.

While I was working it was easy enough to keep out of the Deaners' way. Overtime kept me late at the factory. I went to a restaurant for my suppers. I came in late, went up to my room and read.

But on my second day home again, little Gregory came upstairs to play with me. To tell the truth, he was a plain nuisance to me. I wanted to read, or just lie on my bed looking up at the ceiling. But how can you be rude? I saw my door handle turn, the door opened a little, a face appeared in the crack and stared at me.

I turned over to the wall, but I could feel the stare in my back. Never try to outlast a kid. After five minutes of silence I got up and said, 'Your mummy'll be cross with you.'

From about level with the door handle the clear eyes did not flinch. I saw how velvety dark brown the irises were. He spoke one word, calmly, not a plea or an order, but a simple decree. 'Play.'

'You better get downstairs to your mummy, hadn't you?'

'Play with me.'

'You play in the cupboard, go on. I'm reading a book.'

'You can be the baby tiger.'

'Not today, Gregory.'

He opened the cupboard door. 'You have to get in here.'

'Gregory, your mummy said you mustn't come up here.'

'I'm the daddy tiger and you can bite me.' I was looking at him as unfriendly as I could, but his eyes stayed clear and innocent.

'I'll shut the door and you can play outside quietly.'

I shut it, and turned back to my bed, but I heard the door open behind me and he came in. A child is so sensitive that sometimes one careless word can break his heart. Later I found out that the word 'baby' could do this to Gregory. He ran into a woman in the street, and she shouted at him. I said to her, 'Why don't you leave him alone, he's only a baby.' Gregory waited till she had gone, then his face went scarlet and crumpled up and he started to cry bitterly. I tried to comfort him, but he went on howling, and it was some moments before I heard what he was blubbering—'I'm not a baby. You called me a baby. I'm not a baby.' But at other times you can snub him, insult him, plead with him, reason with him, shout at him, he simply chooses not to hear. He gives you the choice: stop trying or drive yourself crazy.

He held up his hand to me and said, 'You can really bite me. I don't want to bite you back.' He stood there, a little sprat in the corner of my room, making this offer of inconceivable generosity. What can you do?

I put a *Daily Mirror* on my table and said, 'All right, sit down quietly and look at the pictures.'

'Will you be the baby tiger or the daddy tiger?'

I lost my temper. 'Look here, I'm not getting down on the floor. Understand? I got my clean trousers on. I am not going to play tigers with you. No tigers. Understand?'

'What shall we play then?'

I looked round in desperation and saw a pack of cards. 'Look, I'll drop one of these, and you stand next to me and see if you can drop one on top of mine.'

This was a game we used to play with cigarette cards when we were small. After two tries he got the idea. With great concentration, he dropped his third card, then he rolled his eyes up at me, his face shining with innocent cunning, and said, 'You're playing with me.'

After a half-hour we were still playing. All the time I was praying for the sound of his mother's voice. Where was the damn' woman now that I wanted her? It was a strain playing with him. I was tired out. The soft whine of his voice irritated me. There is something in a kid's attitude, the matter-offactness with which he demands, demands, demands, demands, that sucks the marrow out of your bones. I began to understand why his mother was in such a state.

In the end, we heard the street door open and bang shut, and footsteps in the hall. He said, 'That's Mummy,' and at once, forgetting me and the game, he rushed downstairs.

I formed a suspicion about this which was confirmed a couple of days later when I heard his mother go out and a minute later he came upstairs. He knocked at my door this time. He wouldn't have done this unless she'd told him to. I decided on no nonsense. I opened the door and said, 'Go down to the basement, son. Play with Mr Siskin.'

Gregory walked into the room. 'He smells.'

He picked up the cards and said, 'Shall I drop the first one?' I wondered how to get tough, but he said, 'Mummy will soon be home,' and I decided to wait till I could have it out with her.

But she was smart enough to know just how far she could use me, and she came upstairs. 'Oh, Mr Boas,' she said. 'I hope you don't mind. Did he behave himself?'

'Yes, he behaved himself.'

'I wouldn't have let him, but you do seem to be fond of him. I don't know what to do with him, really I don't. I have so much work to do, and he does get in the way. And I can't go out for a minute shopping without wondering what to do with him. It is a blessing to have someone. Are you sure you don't mind, Mr Boas?'

I heard myself saying, 'No, I don't mind.'

'Oh, that is a blessing. I mean, just to have someone. Honestly, I'll be glad when he starts school. If only there was a suitable child he could play with.'

The street was swarming with children.

Anyway, from that day I was in business as child-minder. When his mother wanted to get on with her housework or do a bit of shopping in peace she sent him up to me. Gregory and I got into a routine. We always started off with the card game. Then I taught him 'knocksie-down', which is setting one card up against the wall and flicking others at it to knock it over. Then we invented a bus game, with two chairs, me the passenger, and Gregory either driver or conductor as he fancied. After each game, as I slumped on the bed, came his wail, 'What shall we do now?' In the end he got me playing tigers. I bought a set of snakes-and-ladders to help pass the time. He learned quickly enough, but when a game went against him he would look anxiously up into my face and say, 'Can I cheat, please?' Or he would cheat and then chuckle ecstatically, and cry out in triumph, 'I cheated!'

My name tickled his fancy. He used to call up from the foot of the stairs, in the incredible child's yell that you can hear from the end of a street, 'Harrybo-o-y!'

It was early April now. The weather was fresh and sunny. Sometimes I took him for walks. I never tried to hold on to him like his mother did, but he would slip his hand, tiny yet with skin that when unwashed was as hard as a workman's, into mine. Sometimes he dashed on ahead, hooting and prancing with happiness, but he never ran into the road.

Late one afternoon we were coming in from a walk when he took my hand and said, 'I want to show you something.'

He opened the door of his mother's living-room. He had emptied his toybox and, before coming up to me, he had organised all his toys into a little town. He had made streets with strips of wooden beading, and he had lined them with varying stacks of toy bricks which he identified to me as shops, houses, the school, the hospital, the police station and so on. His miniature cars were set out in rows in the streets, and at the intersection were traffic lights and little lead policemen. On one side of the town was a railway station, with porters, passengers, baggage and trolleys on the platform, and the rails and rolling stock of his train set were laid out beyond. At another place he had his tin garage with trucks and cars waiting to be served at the pumps. He pointed everything out to me, then he knelt over his little city and forgot all about me. He had stepped into a world of his own and now he made it function. Two buses collided. A police car came, then an ambulance to take the passengers to the hospital, then a breakdown van which towed each of the buses to the garage. He wound a clockwork locomotive and let it draw a train into the station. Then taxis stopped at the station, picked up passengers and took them away, setting them down at shops and houses. The policeman moved from the crossroads and took up a position outside the school, where he held up the traffic so that the children could come out in safety. It was all a perfect, minutely-observed imitation of life.

He was absorbed in his town and I was absorbed in him when his mother's voice came from behind us: 'Gregory! Your dad will be home soon.'

She came in and put down her shopping bag. 'Really,' she said to me, 'I don't know what you must think of all this mess in our lounge. Every day it's the same.'

The kid had become mute. His mother said, 'Every day he puts his toys out like this. He won't play with them like other children. He just sits there and you can't get a word out of him. He screams if you touch anything. Don't you, Gregory?'

His lips were clamped together, and his eyes had gone empty.

She said, 'Honestly, Mr Boas, I've tried to bring other children to him and he just drives them away. He sits with all this lot, and he won't let another child touch it. He won't even let us touch it. Gregory! Put them away!'

He did not move. She said to me, 'You see that? I have the same thing every night. Every evening it's a battle. Gregory! I won't have your father seeing the room in this state. Put your toys away or I shall put them all in the box and take them to the hospital for the poor children.'

In silence he began to put the toys away. He did not look at either of us. The little city vanished into the toybox, and as I went upstairs I wondered what had made him create it.

What sort of life could his parents lead, that he was forced to create his own little world of order each day?

And this woman, did she know what she was doing when she made him break it up every night?

CHAPTER SEVEN

On my mantelpiece a twenty-four-hour candle burned for the anniversary of my father's death. Another candle burned in an antique silver holder over Debbie's Adam fireplace. I went to her house in the morning and she fed me a lovely dinner. 'Mother's dinner,' she said, bringing me a king-size plate of motza-meal dumplings in soup, the sweet carrot stew called tzimmas that was my childhood favourite, and apple strudel. There was no conversational nonsense during this meal. I put my head down and fed. She listened to the sound of my eating, head on one side, hands clasped in front of her breast, watching me with love and admiration.

We went to the burial grounds in a Minicab. It was a year since Debbie, on orders from Gus, had taken driving lessons, a time of terror and dismay for her, also no doubt for other people. Gus drove a big Humber, the sort Cabinet Ministers are taken about in. For Debbie he had bought a two-tone Triumph Herald. No shopping car for the wife? In their part of town, a disgrace. As a social necessity the second car had to stand in the garage. But Debbie, trembling and terrified, had failed her test three times and had finally been excused by Gus from further attempts. The girls used the second car and Debbie, reprieved, went on phoning for cabs.

Father is buried at East Ham, a long drive from Finchley. I asked some more about Gus and the girls, as if I cared, and for the whole run I only had to sit back and listen while Deb gossiped and giggled. At fifty Deb still has not only the soft, pure skin of a child but many of a child's innocent ways, making her seem pathetic but also lovely.

She kept up her prattle as we stood at the foot of father's grave. We stood there as if we were waiting for a bus. She finished telling me about an expensive party, mused in silence for a minute over the inscription on the tombstone as if she was reading it for the first time, then gave a dainty little sigh and said, 'Poor father.' She took out her handkerchief and wiped her eyes.

She brightened again. 'Do you remember the farthings?'

When we were small, father used to get a packet of farthings every week from the grocer's shop on the corner. He paid us our pocket money a farthing every day, making three-halfpence by Friday. In the evening, before the Sabbath came in, he gave us the balance, making it up to our weekly threepence, not to be touched again till Sunday. Then we sat down in our best clothes at the table where the candles burned, and the dishes of fried fish and the plaited loaf were laid out on a snowy cloth, and mother stood up to cover her face with her apron and say grace.

I just grunted, 'Yes.'

I didn't want any nostalgia here. Over a grave I feel nothing.

She took my arm and we walked away. 'You were a funny little thing,' she said. 'I can remember you when you were four years old. Mother used to let me do everything for you, I bathed you, I put you on the pot, I used to cut your meat up for you, you were like my dolly. Fancy, I was hardly nine years old, I looked after you like my own baby.'

I let her talk. A little woman, the top of her head level with my chest, she holds the arm of a man rotten with forty-five years, and she sees only a baby. Till she dies she will see me as the innocent baby brother and she will ache with love for me. As long as she is alive one spark of love for me will exist on this earth. The stinking man of forty-five is not real to her, nor is her husband, nor are her daughters. Only the past is real, the ghost of her dead parents that the child recalls. A big joke.

At Mile End the cab turned off our route to town, into Burdett Road.

'I just want to pop in and see a friend,' she said. 'You've got a half-hour?'

And at once I was on my guard, because the guileless Debbie, when she is up to something, has a quaver in her voice that I never fail to catch.

We stopped outside a shop, tobacco and sweets, a smart, fair-sized frontage with a good display. We went in, and Debbie said to the woman, 'Hello, Ray.'

The woman came forward flapping both hands in front of her. 'Why, *hello*, Debbie—' This on a rising note of surprise. 'What a surprise!'

What a surprise! She was wearing a smart two-piece costume—in her own shop on a weekday—pearl eardrops and two diamond rings. No wonder the whitecoated girl assistant looked on ironically from behind the counter!

'Ray, this is my brother Harry. Harry, this is Ray, you know, you've heard us talking about her, she's a cousin of Mrs Gershon.'

She gushed, 'I'm so pleased to meet you. I've heard an awful lot about you, Harry. Come in, please, have a cup of tea. Doris, look after the shop.'

We followed her into the back. Poor thing, she couldn't stop talking. She brought a tray of crockery from the kitchen and an expensive cake from the sideboard. 'Lucky I had the cake. I always have a nice cake in. People are always dropping in. I do like to be ready.'

She asked Deb about Sandra and after a bit of maternity chit-chat she switched her smile at me. 'I should have met you at Sandra's wedding, but I was still in mourning. I couldn't bring myself to go to a wedding.'

Debbie said, 'Ray's husband died two years ago.'

'A tragedy,' Ray said. 'A lovely business we had. A beautiful position, did you see the factory right across the road? Seven hundred pounds a week turnover, forty pounds a week clear profit—'

'And what tax do you pay on a business? Nothing.' This was Debbie.

'A lovely business,' the woman said. 'Did he live to enjoy it? In his sleep the Almighty took him. In a minute. I heard a noise, I thought he was snoring. I pinched his nose, that's what I always used to do when he snored, and it was stone cold. Dead. Mr Boas, I may call you Harry, mayn't I?—let me give you a bit of cake.'

Her eyes were eating me up. I am big for a Jew, five foot ten, bulky but not fat. There is a lot of muscle in me. I am red in the face and nearly bald, but with no jowls and no extra chins. My eyes are blue, my lips thinnish. Mine is the kind of face that looks stronger under a bald head. I stand up straight and I have a trick of looking sharply at people. Also of course I dress well. In short, women know there is a man around when they meet me. This woman was two years without a man. From the plumpness and lift of her body she looked lively and generous, not the kind who can do without it for ever. Her face was honest and good-humoured, though just now anxiety was plain to see behind her smile. And she was young enough to breed kids. Trust Debbie for that. In other circumstances I would have looked her over with at least a moment's interest. Even here, I could have pitied her for the embarrassment behind her eyes. But I hated her for the trap she and my sister had set for me.

Debbie I could not hate, but inside I raged at her. All the time her manner was a dead give-away. Her voice was too animated. A smile of pathetic eagerness was painted on her face. It was painful how she and the woman tried not to look at each other.

Out of the gabble I suddenly heard the woman say, 'I hear you like books, Harry.'

I looked at Debbie. Debbie was staring out of the window as if wonderful things were to be seen there.

Poor woman, I was looking at her as if there was a lump of muck instead of a woman on her chair. Frightened maybe by my black look, she dared not stop. 'I love reading myself. I think it's a wonderful interest. I belonged to a book club for ten years. I took every book. Have you read *Exodus*? I thought it was a wonderful book. I cried. I cried when I saw the film, too. Did you see the film?'

Debbie said, 'Ray is a very cultured person.'

Ray said, 'I always watch the plays on TV. I do like a good drama.'

I said, 'Did Debbie tell you what I do for a living?'

Debbie broke in, 'Ray—you and Harry have something else in common—'

I trod her voice down with mine. 'You must have heard it around the family. I'm a gambler. Gus gives me money, it's like flushing it down the pan.'

Spots of red came in Ray's cheek. She smiled bravely. 'Well, I always say, let a man have his fun. When it's time to settle down, he'll settle down.'

I stood up and said, 'Debbie, I got a date in town.'

That poor widow. She sat behind her tea-trolley, and the scarlet flooded up her face to the roots of her hair. She still smiled piteously at Debbie. She didn't know what else to do. She was still smiling when we left.

We walked towards the cab rank in West India Dock Road. I said, 'A nice shop you found for me.'

She kept silent.

'Grand free offer. A wife with every shop. Get yours today.'

Her mouth twisted, then: 'Did you have to hurt her?'

'A very convenient idea. Did the two families have a conference about it? Or was it just you and Gus? You got a poor relation. They got a poor relation. Marry them off. Perfect.'

'How can you say a poor relation?'

'How long are you going to keep on doing this to me?'

'She's a nice woman. You had no right to hurt her.'

'I told you once and for all. Stop being a marriage bureau. After all these years, haven't you learned?'

'What do you expect? You're my brother.'

'Leave me alone.'

I stopped a cab. We got in and the driver made for town. As soon as we were settled she said, 'You're my brother. We've got no parents. Who else have we got? I worry for you.'

'I do all right, Deb. Don't worry.'

'Who will there be when I'm gone? Who'll look after you?'

'You got many years, Deb.'

'Who knows? Fine young women go, in six months, the hospital and they're gone. Look at Ray's husband, in a second.' She put a hand on my arm. Terror was in her face. 'And I ask myself, what is my brother's future? A gambler.'

'I don't always have to be a gambler.'

'So what then?'

'I'll buy some property one of these days.'

'Property, yes, you told me. When, tell me, when?'

'When I get some capital.'

'How much capital?'

I shrugged my shoulders. 'For a cheap investment, five hundred.'

She looked out of the window. 'Gus won't give any more.'

'I know Gus won't give.'

'He's a good feller, Harryboy. A lovely man.'

'I know he's good.'

Her eyes were brimming liquid. Her mouth moved, and she twisted the fingers of her gloved hands together.

I said, 'I'll get capital. I'll have luck on the track.'

She cried. 'No. Always the track. I'm sick of it. Harryboy, please. Learn. From under the earth I can hear our parents crying.' Tears were spilling out of her eyes. 'Please, darling. Learn.'

'Look, I promise, as soon as I get a win—'

'A win!' She gave a hysterical laugh. 'As soon as the Messiah comes!' She pulled off a glove and tugged at a ring on her finger. 'Here—' The ring came off. She held it out to me. It was a knucker, a three-carat diamond solitaire in platinum. 'You want capital?'

'Debbie, have you gone crazy?'

'Take. Take. Buy houses. Stop crushing my heart. Let my brother be a mensch for a change, a settled man.'

I pushed her hand back, she held it out again. 'Go on, take. I know what I'm doing.'

I showed her my wallet. 'I've got money.'

'Spending-money you've got. Take from me, to start a good life. Harryboy, I love my husband.' She spoke through bitter weeping. 'I'll steal from him and take the sin on me, it'll be a good deed if you make a new start. You can even pay me back one day.'

'Don't you know me by now?'

'You're a good boy. From a little one, you were a good boy. You haven't changed.'

'What would you say to Gus?'

'I lost it, I'll tell him I lost it. I was washing my hands, it fell down the sink. So he'll get the insurance. Harry. Please.'

I closed her hand and forced it back into her lap. Then, for the first time in many years outside of ceremonies, I kissed her cheek. I said, 'Don't cry, Dvorele.' It was our mother's name for her.

The taxi was in Aldgate. I tapped at the window and it drew in to the kerb. 'I'll go into Bloom's,' I said. 'A salt beef sandwich I can't pass by. When you make another tzimmas for dinner, let me know.'

She was sniffling and wiping with her handkerchief. 'Every Tuesday I make a tzimmas, you don't know?' She smiled but another rush of tears rolled down. 'So when else do you have a home meal? With strangers in restaurants you eat, who knows what they give you?'

'Shh! Give my love to Gus and the girls.' I walked away.

CHAPTER EIGHT

A gambler's day goes pleasantly enough. He gets up late, and before he cleans his teeth—if he is as hygienic as all that—he reads the *Greyhound Express*. His first call is at the barber's, where a long session is as much devoted to business—discussing the afternoon's race-cards with the boys, telling them how he got on last night and hearing their stories—as to the pleasure of lying under hot towels. The rest of his day consists of a pleasant mooch from one listening-post to another. These, the places where he can pick up information, include the restaurant or nosh bar where he has his lunch, and also a number of favourite street corners, billiard halls and betting shops along the three-and-a-half miles from Stamford Hill to Aldgate, where the fraternity of the doggies and the ponies gather, the fellows who block the pavement in groups that cluster round opened newspapers, fellows with close-shaved cheeks shining from the barber's razors, spotless belted raincoats or glovetight long black overcoats, good suits, bright ties, smart fresh shirt-collars and sporty trilbies that all look brand-new. A good life, if you're not one of the goomps who think there is some virtue in hard work. In the evening, of course, the tracks.

To this, I added afternoons reading on my bed, and visits to the library. There is a branch library two blocks from where I live, a noisy place. At one end kids scamper round the shelves of their section, shrieking with laughter till the librarian hushes them, uncomfortably quiet for a while, then soon shrieking again. At the other end the housewives chatter, waiting to rush at the librarian like gabbling hens at a fistful of seed every time she comes to the shelves with another armful of 'romances'.

At the end of one afternoon I went in to look for some thrillers. I like these books, the way they scratch on the nerves as I lie in bed. Chandler and Hammett are my favourites. You don't get writing like theirs nowadays. I've read all Mickey Spillane, but he lacks class.

I was looking along the shelves when a fellow came round the end of a bookcase. It was Deaner, the husband. He said, 'Hallo. Seen anything good?'

I said no, and he held a couple of books out. He said, 'I've got these.' Two new novels, fashionable names, the kind that are praised in the highbrow Sunday papers. Every week these papers find another writer who has 'earned his place in the front rank of contemporary writing'. This front rank must be miles long by now. There must be a lot of poor nits like this Vic who are so busy keeping up with this front rank lark that they never have time to read a real book. He said, 'Do you read much?'

I said, 'Not much.'

I knew that tone in his voice. The sentry's challenge of the book-lonely. He stood there waiting for me to give the right password. Among the uneducated (which frankly is what you would call the general population where I live) the serious reader is a lonely person. He goes about among the crowds with his thoughts stuffed inside him. He probably dare not even mention them to his nearest pals for fear of being thought a schmo. There's a hunger in his eyes for someone to talk to. He watches, and from time to time when he sees someone likely, he makes his signals. His situation is very much like that of the nancyboy. I spoke to discourage him. I didn't want him falling on my neck. This Soul Mates idea doesn't appeal to me.

He said, 'I read a lot. When I have time. I sometimes wonder if I've bitten off more than I can chew with this exam. I work at nights till I can't see the figures any more, and I'm still behind the syllabus.'

We looked along the shelves in silence. He said, 'Do you like Upton Sinclair?'

I should have given him the brush-off again, but too quickly I answered him. 'Not all that Lanny Budd stuff. But the early ones are terrific.'

The lights came on in his face and he was gabbling to me like a boy.

So there it was. I never have the sense to keep aloof. The semaphore blinks and I answer it. We moved on along the shelves in silence again, but Vic had a kind of relaxed look, satisfied, like a girl you've assured with a squeeze of the arm. In front of the H.G. Wells shelf we began to talk quite naturally. Wells is an old favourite of mine. This Vic for all his Sunday-papers tastes spoke like an intelligent boy.

I picked up a couple of Simenons, and we walked home together. I had kept out of his way because of that crazy invitation of mine. Now here he was, chatting eagerly, and for all I knew he had forgotten it.

So now you know what I did? All I had to do was to leave it alone. This is what I am always telling myself. Leave it alone. Leave it alone. You're saved. Now stay safe. But something goads me. Words come out of my mouth. Where do they come from?

We went into the house, and in the hall as we were parting, I repeated the invitation. I didn't just repeat it, I pressed it. I said I hadn't forgotten it. We ought to make a date. Now come on. I mean it, you know. Don't be shy.

And having spoken, I waited with an anxious heart for him to shy off. Please God let him at least avoid the issue.

But this time he didn't. His face brightened with hope. He said it was very kind. He'd like to. He'd like to very much. He'd talk to Evelyn, let me know when they could make it.

*   *   *

I came in the next evening. He popped out of his door as if he'd been waiting, and said that any Saturday night would be fine.

I said, 'Let's make it this Saturday.'

'Love to. There's only one thing. We can't both come. We haven't got a baby-sitter. Evelyn says she'll stay in, she says we can go out and have a bachelor party.'

This was no disappointment to me.

I took him to a small Italian place in Soho for lasagne and wine. I was depressed, sick of myself and him. Why brag? And if I had to brag did I need to brag to a schlemiel like this one? He wasn't worth the money.

But he was getting his money's worth. Even going there in a taxi was a treat to him. He leaned back on the stale leather as if he was soaking luxury in through the back of his head. He walked through the Soho streets like a kid at a circus. By my life, his mouth was open. The neon lights in the dusk, the smell of cheese from the delicatessens, of French bread from the bakeries, of coffee and gutter refuse, the girls in the clip-joint doorways, the photos outside the nude clubs, the river of cars gleaming in the narrow streets, the jostle of many people, the Maltese toughs on the corners, the blackies rolling dice in side alleys, the restaurants, the boys and girls crowding into the jazz bars and the juke music pouring out—this fellow was Noddy in Toyland tonight.

We sat down at our table and he said to me, 'I don't suppose you'll believe me, but this is the first time I've been out without Evelyn since we were married.'

'How long is that?'

'Seven years.'

'And Debbie wants me to get married!'

I filled a glass of wine for him and let him talk. He drank the wine as if it was lemonade, obviously not used to it, and I kept filling up for him. Pasta I like to eat seriously, my head down to it, and where there is a plateful of rich gravy as they serve it in this place, my special pleasure is to break up and rip the French bread, mop the plate, let the keen savour of sauce and wine spread from the palate right down to the guts. This calls for silence, for respect.

So I ate, and reached out occasionally for the wine carafe that kept him talking. 'As a matter of fact,' he said, 'since Gregory was born, Evelyn and I never get out at all. We've never been able to find a sitter.'

'I thought your mother lived near.'

'I don't like to bring her out at nights. She's in very poor health. Mind you, I always led, well, a pretty quiet life.' Another swallow of wine to warm his courage. 'That's the wonderful thing about being married. I mean, you've always got someone. I never seemed to make friends when I was single. I never did at school much, really. There was just Mother and me at home. I can't even remember my dad dying, I was very small at the time. It's funny, I can talk to you. I'm not usually much good at talking to people.'

I gave him some more wine. He said, 'I went out sometimes with a couple of chaps from the stockroom at work, you know, just going to pictures at nights. But we never really talked. I stopped going out with them when I got engaged. I used to go rambling as well. You don't really meet people, even though there is a crowd. There just used to be this advert in the local paper, "Meet Dalston Junction Sunday 9 a.m. Bring sandwiches," and you went along, and you had quite a nice walk with them, and all this sing-song stuff on the way, but you never really got to know people. Do you know how I met Evelyn?'

'How?'

'At evening classes. We both went to the City Lit. Appreciation of Poetry. It was something to do in the evening. Do you know how we got talking?'

'How?'

He snickered the first foolish laugh of the mildly drunk. 'Well, I mean me. I couldn't open my mouth to anyone. After each lecture they had discussion. I kept egging myself on to take part, but I couldn't. Everyone else in the class did. Except Evelyn. That's how I noticed her. It's funny how fate works, isn't it? She was the only one I could pluck up courage to speak to, because she was the only other one who couldn't stand up in front of the class. And that's how it all started. Mind you, she's not really shy, Evelyn. Not since we married. Marriage brought her out no end. You should hear her telling off a shopkeeper, or a bus conductor if he's cheeky. I can't tell people off. But my goodness, you should hear Evelyn! I've a great admiration for my wife, she's the brains in our home, really she is. It's her, really, that keeps me at it. I get so tired sometimes, honestly, I could give up and stay where I am, I haven't got such a bad job. But Evelyn's got her eye on the future all the time. Lucky for me she has. She says, "Do you want to be a bookkeeper in a store all your life? Don't you ever want us to be respected? Don't you want a car? Don't you want a nice home in a select neighbourhood?" And I do, I do. If only I had more go. If Evelyn didn't keep me up to it I think I should just be content to go on living in the flat. After all, we're only a few streets away from Mother. It's funny, I was so miserable when I lived at home with Mother, I only wanted to get away. And now I've got my own home, I want to live near her, I'm always going round to see her. They say absence makes the heart grow fonder. Of course, frankly, Evelyn doesn't get on so well with my mother. I'm sure that's another reason she wants us to move. Do you believe in nuclear disarmament?'

'No. I don't care who does what.'

'Oh, I think we all ought to be concerned. Evelyn and I disagree on that subject. We do disagree, you know. Evelyn is very strongwilled, but I do have my own opinions. I told her tonight, "You can't always have your own way. I'm going out." She doesn't like you, you know.'

'I know.'

'It's not prejudice, honestly. She just thinks we should keep to ourselves. She says there'll be time enough to make friends when we move to a better neighbourhood. Am I talking too much?'

'It's good for you.'

'It does do you good to talk, doesn't it? I feel terrific. I love this wine. It tasted sour at first. But I love it. Oh, for a beaker full of the warm south. Harry, I feel so tired. It's pandemonium at the store. It's not like a quiet office. They're rushing in and interrupting you and piling on work all day, and there's all the din from the shop and the traffic in the street. I come home, I can't open my eyelids, my back aches. I could just lie down and sleep for ever. I could die. I could die happily sometimes. Only Evelyn's right. I've got to keep at it. I don't know how I get those books open some nights, let alone memorise the figures and do all those damned exercises. Do you know what I do when I'm tired? I go and look at Gregory in his bed. We bought a little bed for him. He grew out of his cot a year ago. He looks so peaceful and lovely. He looks like a little imp sometimes in the daytime. You know, sulky, or mischievous, or angry, he can look like a little old man when he's angry. But when they're asleep their faces all smooth out, their little fists clench on the cover, they're so beautiful, they look like babies again. I wish he could always stay a baby. I could cry when I look at him. Only I wish I could see more of him. When I come home from work it's his bedtime. And weekends I'm working most of the time. Perhaps I'm just imagining, but he doesn't even seem to take much notice of me. I wonder if I'm just the lodger as far as he's concerned.' His voice failed, and he said, 'I do love him.'

He sat quiet for a minute. Ashamed of himself, I suppose. So I gave him some more wine, and he looked up at me again, and said, 'You mustn't mind Evelyn not liking you. She's a good girl. One of the best. She works so hard. She keeps a lovely house for me. I don't know what I'd do without her. Only she can't always have her way. Can she?'

I waited for the wine to do its work. He said, 'Can she? I mean, look at tonight. I jolly well showed her she can't dictate. Didn't I?' More silence. He held his glass in both hands, looking down into it. Then he took a long swallow. 'She's changed since the baby was born. You know what I mean. She's completely different. She used to be quite, well, advanced. I was surprised when we got married. She wasn't at all shy. You know what I'm referring to.' He paused again. I knew it wasn't going to be for long. Let a weak man start talking about sex, and he can't stop. He's getting his pleasure the easy way. So now it came gushing out. 'I know it's a strain having Gregory in our bedroom. I mean, we do have to be careful. But Evelyn's a fanatic about it. If I try to talk to her, she hushes me up. When we, you know, do anything, she won't take her pyjamas off. The moment the bed creaks she makes us both lie still. Honestly, I just can't do anything when you have to keep your nightclothes on, and you mustn't move, and you mustn't whisper, and you can't even turn on the light. It's awful. Anyway, most of the time she won't do anything, she says Gregory's not sleeping too well, or some other excuse. I just don't seem to have the heart any more. I have read that all the pain and so on in childbirth puts them off it. I feel quite guilty about it sometimes. It does make you feel a brute. She is right, you see. We must get out of this place. For our own sakes as well as Gregory's.'

I sat back, gorged, warm, my chest swelled out with contentment and lordly satisfaction. A man feels good with money in his wallet, and at his best in a restaurant, where all is to command. The waiter stands against the wall, a glance from me and he swoops, to bow at my table and ask respectfully what I will have next. This is the ointment that soothes away all the bruises on my pride, closes the wounds of humiliation, heals my self-respect. I need this. I have to make the most of it. That is why I am at my worst in a restaurant after dinner. A stage is created, I have been given a part to play, and compulsively I find myself playing it. I ordered cigars. The man came with the boxes, and the big act was on. I searched through the boxes, sniffed cigars, crackled them at my ear, smiled like a father at Vic's timid refusal of one, chose a good one and lit it. I leaned back, a king.

'What do you earn, Vic?' I spoke judiciously, gently, leaning on my elbow. Big Executive interviewing applicant.

'Twelve pounds a week. Clear of tax, of course.'

'You can live on that?' Sympathetic, patronising, with no intention to hurt yet knowing the needle I was pushing into him.

'It is a squeeze. Evelyn's a wonderful manager, but Gregory needs so much. His clothes alone! And food! He wants steaks. He screams if we try to economise. He only wants steak. I will say this for Evelyn, she's careful with food, I mean, she thinks it's criminal the way some people indulge themselves with food, but she does like to keep Gregory well dressed. She'll go into the smartest shops and buy him things. Only you see, it's so hard to save. I don't smoke or anything, but I just can't seem to save.'

'You'll never make money working for someone else.'

'I know. I've just got to qualify. Once I'm qualified I'm sure it'll be all right. Company secretaries get to know all the Stock Exchange tips. They can make a real packet.'

'Best thing is your own business.'

He laughed miserably. 'I don't think I'm cut out for that. You have to have a sort of, I don't know, push, imagination, that I haven't got.'

'You got to be able to take a chance.' Listen to the Big Business man talking.

'I couldn't. I could never take a chance. I couldn't sleep at nights.'

'Take gambling. When I was a boy, how old, twenty years old, I was making more than you are, just gambling. And that was on the side.'

'Oh, gambling—'

'Don't say gambling like that. There's gambling and gambling. Of course, you got to be able to take a chance, but you don't imagine I go to the track to give money away to the bookies. The suckers do that. I make a science of it. I study. I know what I'm doing.'

'Do you still gamble?'

I laughed, studied the long ash on my cigar. Oh, Big Time, that was me! 'Gamble? Are you kidding? You don't pay tax on gambling profits, you know. How else can a man live these days?'

'I couldn't do it. I haven't got your courage.' Suddenly he burst out. 'It makes me mad sometimes, honestly. There seem to be two kinds of people. There's such as me, the mugs. You work, what do you get for it? And then I read about these people, some shares go up and they pocket millions. Or these take-over bids. If you're in the know, you just go to a race-track and put money in your pocket. Thousands of pounds it could be. I mean...' He let out a long sigh like a balloon going down. 'Don't think I'm jealous. I haven't got their courage. I haven't got yours. I don't deserve to get on. Only I don't seem to be getting anywhere.'

I took a few puffs of my cigar, sympathetically. 'I'll have to take you sometime,' I said.

'Where?'

'To the track.'

He looked doubtful. 'I think the less I have to do with that sort of thing—'

'It's a spectacle. I wouldn't let you do anything silly.'

He brightened up. 'It would be an evening out. Evelyn would have a fit if she...Not that, I mean...I make up my own mind about these things. It would be an evening out, wouldn't it?' I'd ordered a brandy for him. He finished it, and blurted out: 'You were going to take me to see your houses.'

My lies come flying back at me like bricks. I have learned to duck them without panic. 'Ah, what d'you want to look at a lot of old houses for?'

'I didn't specially. It's just...' He leaned forward, a young, silly smile on his face. 'I do like going around with you.'

I don't know what there was in this appeal that embarrassed me. I heard my own voice, roughly: 'I'll tell you what, we'll go round and have a drink with a woman friend of mine.'

His eyes were unsure. 'I wouldn't like to, er...well, hang around. I suppose I did ought to be getting home.'

'Don't be daft. You come and meet Marcia, have a drink.'

He brightened up again, full of fear and joy. He was going to be shown Life.

While I was phoning Marcia I thought, now, why did I have to say that? I don't know, there was something sickly in the boy's appeal which made me react. I have read these psychology books according to which everybody is queer but doesn't know it, and frankly, I'm sceptical. I never sensed anything queer in this boy, only immaturity, loneliness and tonight unaccustomed drink. And me? What did I have to be proud of? A man of forty-five offloading his sickness on to a little schnip fifteen years younger? At least I could have picked some opposition of my own weight.

Marcia was suspicious. Just because she's friendly sometimes, she doesn't want anyone to make the mistake of thinking she has a soft heart. I asked her to do me a favour, I had a chap with me I was conning for some business deal, I just wanted to bring him in ten minutes for a drink, would she play up to me? She said, What, and find herself in a police court for aiding and abetting? I swore it was on the level. I said I'd stay on for a short time with her, and this could come out of our time. She said, 'All extras are paid for here.' I agreed. Can you beat it? Now I was paying money just to do my act?

The visit to Marcia made Vic's evening. He would live on this for years. He had no idea it was a whore's flat. Not that I blame him for this. The flat is a nice one, nothing flashy, the same goes for the maid, and Marcia herself really looks like one of the County. No, to him it was a ride in a taxi to Piccadilly, a visit to a smart business woman's West End flat, a marvellous glimpse of night life, of the great world.

He murmured his how d'ye do's and sat in a respectful silence. I asked Marcia how the property market was, and she got the idea, and we played it back and forth over the drinks, two successful speculators comparing notes.

Then I showed Vic out. I suddenly realised that he hadn't expected me to stay. He looked at me thunderstruck. It was like a young boy after someone had just shattered him with the facts of life. I didn't wink at him, or mutter any doggish remarks. I just put my hand to his shoulder and ushered him benevolently to the door, and he went in a daze. Now he was hurt. Now he was sick with envy. Now he felt that life, a great mysterious feast—this sleek woman its symbol—was being enjoyed by others, by me. Why was he left out? He smiled his goodnight, but behind it there was the misery of a little boy being pushed out of the children's party.

So this was what I had done to him tonight. I stayed my half-hour with Marcia, and then, since it wouldn't do to follow him home too soon, went to an all-night café in Aldgate (Aldgate, the hub of my world) for eggs and bacon. I let myself into the house at three a.m. I shrugged off what I had done. As usual, I made the old excuse of sinners that I do no harm to anyone but myself. This is never true, as I was to find out.

CHAPTER NINE

April went by. I was seeing a lot of the Deaners. Almost every time I came downstairs, Vic opened the door and called me in for a cup of tea. His wife didn't have much time for me, but I wondered if she had time for anything. Poor girl, she was so determined to make this flat into a preview of the little suburban home of her dreams, that she had turned herself into a kind of domestic machine, which I could hear on the go from morning till night. She was a demon for economising, which was just as well for Vic, on his wages. She was for ever making cushions, knitting, sewing, washing, hunting the shops for bargains, polishing the precious furniture, making curtains for the future house, and doing all sorts of embroidery and fancy work from patterns. She bought 'painting by numbers' sets and hung on her walls the gaudy pictures she made. She always laid her table smartly. She always went out nicely dressed. And she kept the kid spotless. He could get dirty ten times a day, she always had a clean change of clothes to whip on him. I had to admire her.

Every Sunday morning, while Evelyn was busy with the roast, Vic took his little boy for a walk, and I started going with them. When you stay in bed late every weekday, it is nice to get up early on a Sunday morning. Wandering about the streets are large numbers of men turned out till lunchtime by their wives. A good proportion have their dogs to keep them company, and towards midday they drift to join the groups that hang sociably around the pubs, all well-dressed, all thirsting for no more than a respectable pint. The weather was pleasant in those weeks, pale sunshine or breezy with fine showers. We went to Hackney Downs, which is several acres of common land five minutes from Ingram's Terrace. There is a football pitch, and slopes and hollows exciting for children, as I remember, having lived in this district since I was nine years old.

Each week we started off from the house, and Evelyn would stand on the doorstep to watch us go. The little kipper toddled between us, holding both our hands, and over his head we talked. Gregory left us to it most of the time, busy staring at the whole world around him. Sometimes he got jealous, and furiously broke up our conversations, shouting, 'Talk to me. You always talk to each other. Why don't you talk to me?' Once we were in the fields we let him dash away from us like a little puppy.

We really talked it out in those weeks. Or rather, Vic did. He was giving himself a good clearout, as my mother, rest her soul, used to say when she made me take my senna pods. And I can tell you, that man must have been suffering from constipation of the soul for years.

I didn't have so much to say. It was, of course, all bragging. I was giving him a big line about my life on the tracks. God knows what I told him. It wasn't just boasting, it was stories, beautiful stories, with beginnings, climaxes and punch endings. Sometimes I had him shticking, hiccoughing with laughter, wiping his eyes and clutching himself in pain round the waist. All my boyhood spent reading Nat Gould and Edgar Wallace went into those stories, not to mention the Damon Runyon period of my youth. In my time, I gave him to believe, I had seen horses nobbled, dogs doped, jockeys bribed, trainers beaten up, voluptuous females luring secrets out of their bed partners, and in the midst of all this world walked Harryboy Boas, debonair gambler, friend of the famous (oh, yes, I told him how I once lay down on a beach in the South of France, and got a hot tip from the man next to me, who turned out to be Aly Khan. And there was another story about the Duke of Windsor), easy come, easy go with money, frequenter of champagne parties and guest at celebration dinners of oriental splendour.

He believed me, poor goomp. It must have been this that egged me on to unbelievable lengths. I wanted to see how far I could go before he rumbled me. But he never did. Perhaps it was my offhand manner. Perhaps he just needed to believe.

He used to question me about my winnings. As I reeled off the figures I could hear his bookkeeper's mind clicking off totals, and his eyes were as wide as Gregory's were at the sight of a helicopter. Also, in a timid way, he sometimes tried to get me to talk more about women. I could see this was a great mystery to him. He had to know more, the not knowing was worse than the sensual ache. But although I managed in a vague and grand way to leave him with the idea that women galore were one of the perks of a gambler's life, and that Marcia was only one of many magnificent adventures in my life, I would never talk to him in detail about women, not the way he wanted. How could I with a child present? Vic never seemed to worry about the kid. He not only talked about women, but about his own life, and much more about himself and Evelyn, and the whole confessional. He seemed quite unaware that kids hear everything.

So there I was. Pals with the father. Playmate with the son. Only with the mother was I unpopular. You should have seen her, standing on the doorstep watching us go, dour, arms folded on her chest. What went on inside her skull I didn't know, but I was the enemy all right.

*   *   *

One sunny afternoon Gregory and I were coming back from a walk. His father was at work, his mother was out shopping. I had arranged to bring him home for tea before I went out for the evening. The Easter holidays were not quite over, and all day long the street was full of the shouts of children. As we came down the street this afternoon, a crowd of them were playing hopscotch. We stopped to look.

This hopscotch is an institution in the street. When I was a kid we lived round the corner, but we knew the Ingram's Terrace hopscotch, chalked out across the roadway. Today the kids play with spaceguns and swap television comics, but they are also a traditional lot, and they still have the hopscotch. Traffic rolls over it, rain washes it away, it gets tarred over each time the road is resurfaced, but each time, each year for generations the kids have come out and chalked the big square again on exactly the same spot in the roadway, with all its divisions and markings, and the bigger kids teach the little kids the game.

I always feel funny standing there, a big hulk of a grown-up, watching the kids hop from square to square, kicking the piece of stone about, and trying to remember—trying, hardly ever succeeding—what it was like to be a little tich myself, hopping about on those squares. Today it was a proper little United Nations. There were black kids, Yiddisher kids, Cypriot kids and fairhaired little Saxons dotted about like a lot of chesspieces, or scooting around on the pavement. The street kids, as of old, play twenty, thirty at a time. They call themselves 'gangs', but 'tribes' would be a better word, little self-governing human tribes.

Gregory was watching them in rapture. He stood on the edge of the pavement, sturdy, small, chubby-legged in his short pants, holding his arms out in front of him, fists clenched, in a pose of utter wonder. His eyes were large and serious. I got a waft of memory, one of those pangs in the mind that only last for a second, of myself as small as that (but it was in another street, near the docks) and seeing the bigger kids of seven and eight as great, almost grown-up louts whom I feared and adored.

He stepped off the kerb. For a few moments he dared not go any nearer. Then he took another step. Then another. He was afraid to join in, but although he was now getting in the way of the bigger kids, he held his ground. As they ran past him he looked up at them with a timid smile of appeal. Sometimes one of the boys almost ran into him and had to stop, but the bigger ones were always gentle with him. They fight each other like savages but they are unbelievably tender with little ones. One of the 'big boys' (nine years old!) stopped next to Gregory, put a hand on his shoulder, and in the most soft, gentle voice began to explain the game to him. Gregory stood in a daze of worship. When the big boy moved off he trotted after him like a little dog, and a few moments later he was standing on the chalk square, trying to hop about on one leg. Each time he tottered and had to put his other foot down, he laughed exultantly and looked towards me with pride, then forgot me completely in his marvellous world of boys. At first he didn't get the idea, but the big boy who had befriended him shouted, 'Kick the stone,' and he rushed in and tried to get at it, pushing other boys about. In a moment there was a little bundle of them rolling on the road, three of them, including Gregory and a black kid. The others shouted around them, and from the tangle of limbs and glimpsed happy faces there rose shrieks of laughter. It was as harmless and joyful as the play of a basketful of puppies.

'Gregory!' His mother's voice.

'Gregory!' Harder and shriller. She was there by our gate, with her shopping bag.

He took no notice but the other kids fell away—they scatter and quieten down at the first call from a grown-up—and he was sitting there on his own in the road, red-faced and happy.

'Gregory, do you hear me?'

He stood up. I said, 'Come on, boy,' and docile as a lamb he trotted home.

Tightlipped and silent she opened the door for us, and its bang behind us told me what to expect. She said, 'Gregory, I thought I told you not to play with those boys.'

He was still out of breath, and too dazed with joy to take in her mood. 'Mummy, they let me play. Mummy, the big boys let me play with them. I played with the big boys, Mummy.'

'I told you not to play with them. Didn't I? Answer me. What's the matter, haven't you got a tongue? Are you going to take notice of me? Answer me. What did I tell you?'

His joy died away. Sulky, he lowered his voice. 'Harryboy let me.'

I said, 'It was my fault.'

She kept at the kid. 'I'm not going to let Harry take the blame. You're a big boy. You're big enough to understand. You've got to take notice. Do you hear? You take notice of your mummy and your daddy, do you hear? No one else. You'll take notice of us.' She was talking at him but she meant it for me. 'Harry's not your mummy or your daddy. Is he? Harry's very good to you. Don't take advantage. If you don't behave yourself I won't let you see him any more. Do you understand? I'm not going to burden him with a naughty boy like you. Do you hear? Look at me! Look at me!' She was starting to shriek at him. 'Answer me when I talk to you!'

He stood there with his head bowed. She said, 'I won't have you playing with those dirty boys. Do you hear me? You're not to play with them. I've told you before. They're rough boys. They're different from you. You mustn't play with them. I don't care what anyone else tells you. *I'm* telling you. Your mummy.' The more hysterical she got, the more he glowered, giving out that air of I-don't-even-hear-you with which small kids can drive adults to despair; and this made her even worse. She shouted, 'Answer when you're spoken to. I'll make you listen. I'll make you take notice. You'll take notice of this, won't you?'

She bent down and slapped her hand hard across his face. He looked up at her and I could see she was taken aback, because, instead of the woe or outrage she expected, there was a scowling grin of derision. I walked towards the stairs. What could I do? I couldn't say anything, I couldn't interfere between a parent and child, I mustn't do anything to weaken her authority in his eyes. As I turned away he slapped her leg and shouted back at her, 'You didn't hurt. I can hurt you. You can't hurt me. You're not strong enough.' Then he rushed away from her and up the stairs after me, and he clung to my leg. I stooped down to pick him up and give him back to her. He put his small strong arms round my neck, demanded, 'Kiss!' and smooched a long hard kiss on my forehead.

His mother wrenched him away and glared at me. She panted, 'That's enough!' This was to me. Then, covering up, she babbled on to the child, 'I won't let you bother Harry. Do you hear?'

She ran across the hall with him, pushed open the door of the front room in which they slept, bundled him in, slammed and locked the door. For a moment there was silence inside. She shouted at the door, 'Now you can stay in there till you're sorry. Do you hear?'

Then the kid began to cry. He set up a long dismal howl, which went on for an astonishing number of seconds, then repeated it again and again. This did not break my heart. Crying is a fine art with kids. They look at you, judge how much is needed, then start the performance. Sobs, pathetic whimpers, heartrending shrieks, pitiful moans, all these are let loose till you feel as guilty and miserable as if you'd done murder. Then you give way and in an instant the tears have stopped, the child is victorious.

Against this background Evelyn said to me, in a tired voice, 'You've got to teach them.'

I said, 'Yes...I'm sorry.'

'Nothing to be sorry for. You're not responsible, it's between him and his parents. He's just got to learn.' She sighed, as the shrieks grew louder, and gestured at the door. 'They're so *cruel*. Can't he see how tired I am? You'd think he'd have just a little love.' She took an empty bag from the hallstand. 'I've got to go out again.' Her voice was self-excusing now. 'I shan't be long. I'll give him his tea when I come back.'

She went out, and I went upstairs, and from the room downstairs came shrieks of astonishing, thunderous strength, and the thuds of a small solid creature hurling itself about, and quiet interludes when he just moaned, 'Mummy, Mummy,' in a surrendering voice. And then, when I went out, silence from the bedroom.

*   *   *

There is an Italian restaurant by Dalston Junction where they serve good steaks. Going there, I crossed the High Street. It was five o'clock, when the traffic was getting heavy. Cars, lorries, buses filled the main road like jammed convoys. I had to wait at the crossing, then scuttle across under the bonnets of threatening vehicles with a crowd of other people. I have a reason for telling you this.

I walked down on the other side and was held up at the next lights by heavy traffic. I crossed another street, bought a paper and stepped into the cinema doorway on the corner to glance at it.

I was half-way down the Clapton race-card when a man's voice said, 'Here, mister.'

I looked up. This fellow was standing there, a bus driver still in his heavy winter greatcoat. 'Here, mister,' he said. 'Is that your little boy?'

I looked across the road. There on the kerb, with people round him and others stopping, was Gregory. He was pointing at me.

'Is that your little boy?' I couldn't speak. I was so dumbfounded I couldn't think straight for a moment. The kid was over there, pointing at me. People were bending down speaking to him.

'You want your head examined,' the busman said. I started across the road. The man followed me. 'Letting a kid his age on his own in the traffic. You want reporting, you do. You want your name taken.'

A woman was saying to Gregory as I got there, 'Who's your daddy, sonny? Is this your daddy?'

Someone else said to me, very hostile, ''Ere, is this your little boy?'

I stooped down. Someone was saying, 'Of course it's 'is little boy.'

Gregory was looking at me guilelessly. I began, 'What the hell is this—?' but his arms were around my neck and he was doing that big kiss act again. Proper chorus now. 'Ah, bless him, he loves his daddy.' 'Don't deserve a kid like that, you don't.' 'Someone ought to report it, letting him out in this traffic. No wonder there's all these accidents.' I was squatting on my haunches muttering at the kid, 'How did you get here? Did you tell these people I was your daddy?' He just gazed at me with clear eyes.

I stood up. 'Who found him?' I asked. 'Did he say I was his daddy?'

'He pointed you out,' the busman said. 'He was frightened to speak, poor little nipper. He was here, on this side of the road, and he was looking across at you like a little lost soul. He pointed you out the minute I asked him where his mummy or daddy was.'

'It's a bleedin' shame,' the woman said. 'Poor little lamb.'

'You want reporting,' the busman said. 'Someone ought to take your name.'

'I don't know what it's coming to,' someone else said. 'The way people leave their kids nowadays.'

Gregory stood there, a picture of innocence. I said to him, 'Come on.'

I took his hand and marched him away.

*   *   *

He trotted contentedly at my side. 'Did you tell them I was your daddy?' I asked. 'What you tell them I was your daddy for?'

But he was looking all round him, at shop windows, passing dogs, cars, the whole world.

'How did you get out?' I asked. 'Your mummy locked you in. Is your mummy home? Did she let you out?'

He strained at the end of my arm towards a shop window and I had to wait till he had examined a display of toys. Then, as if I was a dog on a leash he trotted on, towing me.

'Did you cross these roads on your own?' No answer. 'Did anyone take you across? You must never cross roads on your own. D'you hear? Never.'

I had a picture of him trotting after me—heaven knows how he'd got out of the house—this tiny urchin plunging across the two main streets through that crawling, roaring mass of great vehicles, marching along through the tall crowds on his tiny little legs, not stopped by anyone because he looked so determined, so obviously going somewhere, following me. Me! Why, how, mystified me. But by God, it was an epic!

'Gregory,' I wheedled. 'Be a pal, tell me. Tell me, what happened?'

He stopped. His nostrils were lifted to the savoury smell of frying meat. We were outside a Wimpy Bar. He said, 'I'm hungry.'

'Are you? Well, come on, I'll take you home.'

'I'm very hungry. I'm so hungry I shall fall down.'

'You're not getting anything out of me mate. Home.'

'Plee-ease,' he whined.

'Come on.'

'Plee-ee-ease.' I pulled and he pulled back. The strength of a small boy can be astonishing.

'I'll buy you one Wimpy,' I said. 'Will you be a good boy then and come home?'

'Can I have orange juice?' was his only answer as he trotted in, and climbed on to the high stool. I ordered. He was looking round. He said loudly, 'Why is that lady putting powder on her nose?'

'Ladies like powder on their noses.'

'My mummy—' this was even louder, an announcement to the whole shop '—used to put powder on my dinkle.'

The girl brought his Wimpy. I told him to eat it.

He said, 'Does that lady put powder on her dinkle?'

I said, 'No.'

He pondered, while he took the meat out of the wimpy and pushed the bread away in disdain. He clutched the lump of meat between grubby, juicy paws. 'I see,' he announced, giving his conclusions loud and clear for the benefit of all. 'Ladies has powder on their noses, and babies has it on their dinkles.'

I got him out of there. He marched at my side, full of conversation now, a little man of the world. I wiped his hand with my handkerchief, but inside mine it was still sticky with gravy. He said, 'Miss Gosling is mean. She won't give me any sweets.'

I asked again, 'Gregory, is your mummy at home?'

He suddenly wheeled right into my path, and said, 'See how high I am.'

I measured the top of his head against me. 'You're a big boy. How did you get out, son?'

'I'm nearly five.' He was quiet for a moment, then 'Harryboy—?'

'Yes?'

'Does your mummy and your daddy fight?'

'No.'

'Do you get frightened when they fight?'

'They don't fight.'

'But if they did, would you get frightened?'

'No.'

He trotted on a couple of steps. 'I'm not frightened.'

Poor little sprat. He went on a few more paces. 'Why hasn't my daddy got a lot of money?'

'Some people have and some haven't.'

'But you have got a lot of money.'

'How do you know?'

'My daddy told my mummy. Why have you got a lot of money?'

'Sometimes I got a lot and sometimes I got none.'

'Do you know what my mummy told my daddy?'

'No, son. You tell me how you got out of the house, eh?'

'My mummy told my daddy he would have some money if he was a man. But he does wear trousers. He is a man, isn't he?'

'Of course he is.'

'Then why does my mummy think he is a lady?'

'She doesn't. She was joking.'

'I don't think she was having a joke. She was crying. They was in bed.'

'Gregory, son, listen. You mustn't tell people about Mummy and Daddy.'

'But I can tell you.'

'Not me either.'

'But Daddy tells you, when we walk in the fields.'

Those little ears! They hear everything! Everywhere! His father should only know.

To divert him I said, 'I bet I know how you got out of the house.'

He said, 'You don't. I will show you.'

When we got home his mother wasn't back from her shopping yet. And he showed me the secret. The front room, the room he'd been locked in, has a bay window. His mother had left it open about two inches at the bottom. It happens that this window runs very free on its sash—when I tried, I pushed it up with a finger. He had stood on a chair, pulled up the window, and dropped three feet from the ledge into the front yard. The little film in my head was complete. I saw him doing all this and trotting up the road and after me.

He climbed in through the open window and I closed it on me, and he grinned at me, flattening his nose against the pane, then he pulled a mock grimace of woe—the sad little prisoner again, waiting for Mummy to come home and let him out.

But before he climbed in, he said to me, sitting on the windowsill with his little legs sticking out in front of him, 'Harryboy—' he put on his limpid look of appeal—'will you tell my mummy?'

'I must tell her.'

'Please don't tell my mummy.'

'You mustn't have secrets from your mummy, son.'

'Please!' They can stretch it out like a piece of music, that high clear whine of entreaty. 'Please, Harry, please.'

I didn't want to be involved. I didn't want to come between a child and his parents. Waiting there to close the window and fool his mother, I was already his accomplice. Look what he'd done today, he was hanging himself round my neck, like the Ancient Mariner's albatross. I didn't want it. The big eyes and the thin little voice kept on pleading, 'Plee-ease!'

I put my hands on his shoulders. 'Gregory, you been a very naughty boy. You could have got run over. You mustn't climb out of windows and you mustn't go in the street on your own and you must do what your mum tells you.'

'I won't do it again,' he said. His eyes gleamed with a great thought. 'I tell you what—*if* you don't tell my mummy I will be a good boy.'

His face was so transparent, it was heartbreaking. He said, 'If you tell her, I will be a very bad boy.'

He was small and alone and he needed someone. Who did he have? I said, 'You promise you'll be a good boy?'

'I do promise.'

Having got his way, he scrambled inside without another glance at me, and I closed the window on him.

So now I had a guilty secret with him.

CHAPTER TEN

Vic kept telling me how much he'd enjoyed our evening out. 'My treat next time,' was his way of reminding me that we had another date.

So I took him to Harringay. Out of consideration for his pocket I kept him away from the restaurant. I let him pay at the turnstile and buy the first round of drinks in the bar, which we made our base.

In the bar I got a hot tip. It wasn't on the dogs. A geezer I met occasionally round the tracks, I've known him since I was at school, came across and bought us a drink, and we talked about the old East End days. He said the only one of his family left down there now was an uncle, an old shoemaker who kept a shop in Cobb Street, a little turning off the Highway. I said I remembered the shop from forty years ago, and this geezer said, 'Well, it won't be there much longer. The old feller's selling out. He's going into the Old Folks' Home at Brighton.'

'Who's he selling to?'

'Anyone who'll offer him a price. Place like that, you can buy it for the price of a good suit.'

'House to go with it?'

'Sure, he sublets upstairs. There's six years' lease left before they pull it down. Why? You interested?'

'I could be. I got some property down there.' He gave me the address and I wrote it down. A feeling came to me that this was my break. Also I enjoyed doing this in front of Vic.

I was in no hurry to bet. From time to time I get that evening-off feeling. I like to stretch myself, mooch around the track, feel no more than an onlooker, untouched among all those strained crowds. For a change I see the bright, tawdry scene like an outsider, and I enjoy it. On a late spring night you see it against a changing background. The chains of lights, the unearthly floodlit green of the turf, the stir of people, the soft excited hubbub out of which rises the characteristic noise of the track—a yapping tumult from the bookies' stands—it all goes on like a pageant. And in the oval bowl of the arena, in the sky beyond the stands, the pearly evening light dulls to dusk, and the grey dusk gets denser, and blue seeps into it, till you see the bowl of stands and terraces and the mosaic of tiny faces in a smoky darkness shot with lights.

Vic went for all this big. I kept him down to two-shilling Tote bets. I said, 'Save your money, boy. You can get as much fun for two bob as you can for a fiver.'

'Sure, Harry,' he said solemnly. 'I'm not here for the money.'

He was seeing another bit of Life. By courtesy of me.

Our first bet was on the third race. We put our money on the second favourite. Vic had virgin's luck. The dog won.

He followed me for two more races. I showed him how to do a forecast and a reverse forecast, and the reverse bet won.

Beginners always win, and they always react the same. They get wildly elated. They fill with conceit and all of a sudden you can't tell them anything. There floods into them the feeling that they are at home here, that they're enjoying themselves, and like kids they want to show that they're big boys, they don't need you any more. There were three good dogs in the sixth and I told Vic to try a combination, which means that if any two of your three dogs come first and second, you win. Not that boy. He wanted it straight, the winner. And he knew. He pointed to a dog and said this one was going to walk home. He knew, poor goomp! Yes, he did know. He won.

He was crazy now. Laughing, flushed. He swaggered about like an old hand, told me airily he was just popping up to the Tote, and rubbed in what an old hand he was by talking about 'the Two Dog' and 'the Three Dog' instead of 'Number Two' and 'Number Three'.

I said, 'All right, boy, all right. Keep it down.' It is not nice for a beginner to do his nut when he is standing on a terrace full of gamblers, the real sweat-blood brigade, who are losing their week's wages in an atmosphere of grim, respectable quietness.

Just before the last race he vanished. I was too bored to put money on. I bought myself a Scotch and a ham sandwich. People were going home, and after the race ended the stand started emptying out faster. Still Vic didn't appear.

Then he came running. He was like his own kid, almost tumbling over with excitement. Like a kid, he was in that feverish state when tears are only a few seconds away. He shouted to me, 'I won. I won. I won.'

'So you won,' I said.

'You don't understand. Look!' He pulled a fistful of notes out of his pocket. 'Fourteen pounds. I won fourteen pounds. They gave me this. I won.'

I said, 'What did you have on?'

He said, 'A pound, I was fed up with favourites. I had a hunch about this outsider—'

'You had a hunch about an outsider?'

'He won, didn't he?' The boy was still panting. 'It was an instinct, I tell you, I knew.'

'You knew! Put your money away, before one of the whizz artists decides to take it off you. Come on.'

'Whizz artists?'

'Pickpockets.' We were on our way out. 'Vic, I'm delighted you won. It's made a nice evening. Only don't get the wrong idea. Everyone has luck the first time. After that the bookies start taking it back from you.'

'Oh, I know. I know. I wouldn't come again.'

'You were only going to bet two bob. You put a quid on.'

'It was just once. It was just for fun. You've got to have a go once in your lifetime.'

'All right, boy. Only remember. You've had your once.'

'Oh, you won't catch me throwing money away. I wouldn't come again, I mean, not to bet. I'd just watch next time. It is exciting. I am glad we came. You won't catch me betting again, though.'

'You stay at home, boy.'

'Oh, lord,' he said, joyful and scared at once, 'I wonder what Evelyn will say about this lot.'

We were going down the steps. A party of people ambling down in front of us shrank together to make way. They were a respectable bunch, not track people but the sort who came for a dinner and an evening's giggle. Even from behind I could spot them, three solid business men and their hausfraus.

As we passed them, one of the men glanced my way. After twenty-three years I recognised him at once. There was a jolt of shock in my chest. I was going to hurry past but he reached out to touch my sleeve. 'Excuse me,' he said. 'Aren't you Harry? Harryboy Boas? Don't you remember me? I'm Benny. Benny the trumpeter.'

His party were waiting for him as we came down to the foot of the steps. 'I thought it was you,' I said. 'It's been a long time.'

'It certainly has,' he said. 'Still, you always see people again. Many times I've said to the wife, "Years it can be, you always see them again." How are you, Harry? You're looking well.'

I said I was fine and how was he. He said, 'Fine, fine. I'm in furniture now. My own factory. We come a long way, Harry, eh? You too, I can see. What are you doing?'

Being me, I answered, 'Property.'

'Very nice,' he said. 'That's the game these days.' He wanted me to meet his wife and friends. I said another time, I had to hurry. He was puzzled, then he said, 'Well, ring me, then. I'm in the book.'

'Me, too,' I lied.

I was turning away when he said, 'By the way, Harry, do you have a family?'

I said, 'A family?'

He laughed. 'I always wondered if you'd settled down with that nice French girl? What was her name? Very nice girl. So, did you?'

I said, 'I'm not married. I'll see you, Benny.' I walked away.

Benny was right. People always turn up again.

*   *   *

There is where I should tell you about it. In 1938, Benny and I went over to Paris. We lived there for a year. We were young, free, it was the kind of thing boys do in their wild years. He played his trumpet, I played the tracks, and we had the sort of good time boys go to Paris for.

We lived in a dingy hotel in the Rue des Martyrs. I got up late. I spent my days in the betting bars, and at night usually ended up in the cheap night club where Benny played. I learned some French. We slept around with the hostesses. Benny (Ah, that solid business man I saw at the track. I wonder if he remembers?) got the clap for a few weeks. This was our good time.

I used to eat in a family restaurant near the hotel. The cashier there was a girl named Nicole. She was the first straight girl I got to know in Paris. We went around for a while, then we moved into a room together.

She was a serious girl. She was not the sort that got into bed with any fellow. I don't know what it's like now, but in those days I got the impression in Paris that a lot of very nice girls who were on their own and didn't earn much were ready to live with their men friends. It was a question of two being able to live as cheaply as one. Different countries have different ways, and nobody seemed to think the worse of them. Anyway, Nicole took me seriously. I don't think she would have done it otherwise. And she was a lonely girl. She had no family in Paris. She was a Jewish girl, though, oddly enough, the subject didn't come up till after we'd met several times.

I was comfortable with her. She was a good sort. She didn't try to stop me gambling. She took me as I was. I came and went when I wanted to. Whenever I came home she was sitting there in our room, sewing or reading. Apart from my gambling we lived quietly. We had our meals in the restaurant, we went to the pictures once a week, some nights we stayed in our room reading books. Not being a Don Juan, I left other women alone.

She seemed contented with the life. As for me, I was fixed up, as they say. I liked the neat look of her. I had a warm pleasant feeling for her. She used to talk quietly, not a lot, but all her comments were shrewd and sensible. Her eyes were intelligent. I enjoyed going out with her and coming home to her.

But you can't live with a woman like that for a year without questions taking shape. They are never spoken—she was not the sort to make demands—but they are in the air. What was to come of all this? She was a serious girl. She wouldn't be living with me if she didn't have hopes. All the little things she did for me, the way she smiled at me sometimes or took my hand, I'm not such a fool that I couldn't read the signs.

To tell you the truth, I didn't know what I wanted to do. It only needed a word spoken and I would have been committed to her. I dreaded that the word might slip out one day. Yet often I thought, 'Why not?'

Benny went home to England in August. I never saw him again till that night I have just described at the stadium. Every time I thought of my relations with Nicole, I ended by putting the problem out of my mind. But I knew that if I went on living with her I would drift into marriage.

Two days before war was declared—September 1st, 1939—I heard that the British were mobilising and it suddenly seemed natural to make the break.

I left for London on the night train. Nicole was quiet. Those intelligent eyes looked at me but she said nothing reproachful. I felt very bad. I didn't know what I wanted. While we stood on the platform I only wanted to say I would marry her. But once the train was steaming out of Paris I felt a great load lifting from me.

So that was that. On Sunday war was declared. Like a lot of gambling boys, I went on the run. That doesn't mean I deserted. I just moved from one town to another, as long as there was a dog track close by. The authorities couldn't catch up with me, and since no call-up notice could be served on me, I couldn't be accused of desertion. I didn't keep in touch with my mother. If the police called on her, she could truthfully say that she had no idea where I was. I wouldn't involve her by letting her know where I was, even though my disappearance must have caused her a lot of grief. All this was during the so-called phoney war, when nobody took the whole thing very seriously.

In July, 1940, I went home to my mother's. This was after Dunkirk. The atmosphere was different. While the old lady was hugging me I could already see the official envelopes on the mantelpiece. It was my call-up notice, for the Fusiliers. I went like a lamb a few days later.

There were also two other letters—from Nicole. The first was dated from the previous October, and said that she was pregnant. She was a girl with pride and she must have forced herself to wait for several months before she wrote again. The other letter was dated March. It was restrained, just what I would expect from her. No fuss. She just wrote she was worried that the first letter might not have reached me, what with all the wartime difficulties, and she asked me to let her know if I had received it. After that there were no more letters.

Well, it was too late to do anything about the letters by the time I read them. I was off to the Army, for six years as it turned out. And two months before, the Germans had occupied Paris. I already told you, Nicole was a Jewish girl.

*   *   *

I couldn't sleep that night. The meeting with Benny had churned up a lot of memories that kept my mind busy.

What could I have done? Did I know she was pregnant when I left her? In all those months did I know she had written to me?

I wanted my freedom. Was that a crime? There was no understanding between us. She didn't reproach me when I left her. She had nothing to reproach me for.

This was me excusing myself. But then I would become my own accuser. 'So? After the war? How hard did you try to find her, the woman who had your baby?'

So the inside of my head, not for the first time, turned into a courtroom.

The woman who had my baby? How do I know she had my baby? It might have been a false alarm. She might have had a miscarriage. She might have had an abortion. She was the sort of practical girl who would think of such a thing.

Then came the cross-examination about how hard I tried to find her. But I did try, I pleaded. After the war.

Yes, I tried. But not so hard. I left it for a year. I kept finding reasons for waiting a little longer. Maybe I was afraid I'd find myself a wife and child waiting for me. Me, Harryboy Boas, the lone wolf! In the end, on a holiday, I stopped off in Paris—ah, the prosecutor was scathing about this, that I should wait till I was on a holiday—and made some enquiries in the street where we used to live. The hotel had changed hands. The restaurant was gone. No one knew what had become of her. I told myself there was no more I could do. God help me, again I felt that load lifting from me. I went on my way. And that was the last I did about it.

But there were records offices, shouts the prosecutor. Millions and millions were murdered, but they traced and searched for years, they did miracles, they traced victims, they traced survivors. I answer him that I knew nothing about records offices. I did my best.

Did your best? And then forgot her? Don't you know what happened there in Paris? Don't you know what was done to men and women and children? Children, do you hear that, children?

No, in the wartime I didn't know. Who realised, when we were fighting for our own lives, what was happening? Who realised, till years after, when all those books started coming out? Believe me, I've read plenty of those books. I've had plenty of nightmares from them.

The truth is, on this subject I am a man of two minds. Once in a while, when something has happened to upset me, I think for a few hours, I let a nice girl down, maybe she died because of me, maybe a child of my own died because of me.

But most of the time I don't think about it. And when I do, I tell myself my conscience is clear. In the first place, I only lived with her. It was just an arrangement. I had no responsibility. In the second place, she may never have had a baby at all. A thoughtful girl like her in wartime would most likely have got rid of it. In the third place, she might have escaped. She was the sort who could look after herself, wasn't she? I could imagine her joining the Resistance movement. She had the courage. They would have looked after her. Or they might have smuggled her and her child, if she had one, out of Paris. A lot were saved that way. At this very moment she may be living in France, or in America, or in Israel, a middle-aged woman with a husband and a family. She would not have thanked me if I'd tried to trace her. To her, I am probably an episode best forgotten. I would be an intruder, the last man she would want to see. So I tell myself that if, please God, she is alive, I am doing her a good turn by putting her out of my mind. And after all, to be honest, I am best off alone. I can waste my time, waste my life, do what I like. Nobody else is involved. For a long, long time I had not even thought of her. Till Benny bumped into me at the stadium.

The room was hot. I was a million miles away from sleep after all my thoughts. I smoothed out my bed and went down to the bathroom to sluice my face.

I was coming out of the bathroom when I heard someone creeping about downstairs. A shaky, subdued voice, Siskin's, came up to me. 'Who is it? Who is it? Who is up there?'

I went down. He was clutching the banister at the bottom, huddled in a moth-eaten dressing-gown.

'So what are you doing?' I said, 'going round at three in the morning?'

'I thought I forgot to bolt the door,' he said. 'I came up to see.'

'Had you forgotten?'

'No. But I was worried. Burglars,' he said. 'Everywhere burglars these days.'

This man has got nothing. Like a rat in the cellar he lives. His obsessive fear is burglars.

'What have you got for burglars?' I said.

'When you got nothing is worst. With iron bars they hit you.'

'You should worry. Say a prayer. Sleep easy.'

'Who to, a prayer?'

'You're a Jew?'

'Someone looks after Jews? Since when? Tell me.'

'In God you don't believe now?'

'God? Excuse me, I don't know this gentleman. He looks after people? If this is his job he must be the biggest messer in creation.'

'Go to sleep, Mr Siskin.'

'Millions are murdered. I should believe in God? Boas, listen. Above this earth is nothing. On it is only wild beasts. Men. Men are wild beasts. Shouldn't we know? Let them all drop dead—'

'So what is this to do with burglars?'

'Burglars? They come and break your head in. For nothing, your head they break in. Boas, I give you advice. Keep your door locked.'

'I give you advice, Siskin,' I said. 'Go to bed. It's after three o'clock.'

I went back to my room. I was too tired to sleep, so after an hour I took codeines and I was like a dead man till midday.

All this time I was building myself up a not bad bank-roll. On the dogs it was so-so, but I was also betting on the horses with this bookie in the High Street, Ockley, and with him I was lucky.

With a couple of hundred in my wallet I could buy my first house. I could already see myself collecting rents. I even began to change my mind about marriage. Debbie was right, at forty-five a man should settle down. It gave me pleasure to play a scene in the little private cinema I keep at the back of my mind. In this scene I go to Debbie's on a Tuesday and eat one of her tzimmas dinners. It is a wonderful meal and I eat through it deliberately, saying nothing till the last big slab of lockshen pudding is digested. Then I push the plate away and casually say, 'I picked up a nice little snip, Deb. Remember in Cobb Street, the old shoemaker?—' for I had not forgotten the tip at the track. This was the move I had in mind. '—I bought his house. Five years' lease to go.' Debbie claps her hands together like a child. She says, 'Thank God, Harryboy, you made a start. Only don't go any more to the tracks.' I answer grandly, 'You think I'm a fool? Listen, this house is a dustheap, a ruin, but at least it brings me five hundred a year rent. For two hundred capital, I can't grumble. So how long will it take me to get another house? And then another?' And even, in this dream, Debbie screws up her courage and says, 'Harry, dear, if you're going to settle down, you should settle down properly. Won't you look around? You know what I mean. There are plenty of nice women.' I sip my lemon tea, and I say to her, 'Sure, Deb, sure. You think I'm not going to marry? But what's the hurry? A man has time till he's fifty, till he's fifty plenty of women will run after him. So let's look around, find something nice. Deb—you know anyone who can make a tzimmas like you? Show me, and I'll marry her.'

Why not? I am like other men. I play another reel of film in my cinema. I am married. I cannot see my wife's face but she is plump and comfortable. I have a nice house in the suburbs. Not like Gus's, smaller, but pleasant, with a green tiled roof and a shaved lawn in front and a Zodiac in the garage. I want these things. I want them. Many a rich, respectable, religious man was a lowlife till he settled down. Why not me?

Only, one thing is strange. When I am in this mood, I dream of the home, I dream of the woman, I dream of the car, I dream of the business—but never of the children. In my dream they never come to life. In my dream there is only one child. And this is due to a strange trick of the mind.

You see, for all I put Nicole out of my thoughts, one idea sticks. Buried deep inside me is the idea that she did have a baby, and that the baby was a boy. It is so far down that I can't get rid of it. I can forget it most of the time. But it's there.

I suppose it's these books I have read. I know what was done to thousands and hundreds of thousands and millions of children. Once you have read about those trains creeping across Europe with their trucks crammed with terrified, tormented kids being taken to the slaughter, I don't see how you can ever forget. I have only to see a nursery school teacher leading her procession of toddlers to the park, and at once I imagine a procession of little innocents, endless, endless, being herded with every possible cruelty to their deaths. If I walk into the Deaners' living-room and see a pair of Gregory's shoes in the corner, I think of the mountain of children's shoes, the shoes of dead children, found in one of the camps, sixty feet high.

It's no use telling myself that there may not even have been a baby. Sooner or later the idea comes back to me that there was, and that it was a boy. And then I work out the dates on which the butchery started, and I think that my baby boy could have been murdered any time between his second and his fourth year. Think of that. Just you look at some kiddie of two, three or four that you know, and imagine that being done to him.

But then I tell myself that even if there was a baby boy he probably escaped, in which case he is a young man in his twenties now. I'm not interested. I feel no pride in the thought of having a fine upstanding son. I'm not one of those Jews who want sons to say the mourner's prayer over their coffins. If there is such a fellow about, I don't want to know him. It's only the baby, the little one that I think of (when some trick of the mind forces me to think of it at all). A baby who perhaps was murdered in his mother's arms, or even alone—for they often sent the children away on their own, a cute Teutonic refinement. A baby whose father was not there to help him.

And I'm confessing now, however strange it sounds, that when once in a while I do weaken and think of a wife and home, then before the children come into my mind, in marches this little one, as jealous as any living child, and he won't let the others in.

So anyway, it was May already, and I went down the East End to look at this house. The old shoemaker was gone. Most of the shop window was boarded up and the small window left in the middle was curtained. A Pakistani family lived inside. Judging from what I could hear, there was also a fair boatload of Pakistanis living in the upstairs rooms. On the off-chance I asked about the landlord. The man at the door couldn't understand much I said, but from his reaction to the word 'landlord' I should say it was one of the first half-dozen words he had learned in English. He pointed across the road to a café, and said, 'Ali.'

'I want the landlord,' I repeated.

He repeated 'Ali.'

'Ali the landlord?'

'Landlord, yes, landlord.'

Which was clear enough. The café was one of those old gaffs with a sunken doorstep, a passage at the side leading to a wooden staircase at the back and a yard with an outside lav and dustbin, both of which you could smell from the street (and inside while you were eating). The café was nice and shady inside, although it was a sunny day, because the window hadn't been washed since, I should judge, the last English tenant left at the time of the blitz. There were three pairs of marble tables, a dirty floor, posters on the wall advertising Pakistani films, a counter at the back covered with slopped oilcloth and a door leading to a kitchen from which came a smell of spicy cooking. This was overlaid by a smell in the café which was like asthma cigarettes. Reefers, maybe.

Three West Africans sat at one of the tables rolling dice. None of them spoke. No money was in evidence. None of them moved except for the turn of the hand to cast the dice. They just sat there like statues with black, sharp faces carved from anthracite, their eyes gleaming inwardly, as if they were doing it only to hear the rattle of the dice on the marble table. Behind the counter was a little chip of an Indian in a powder-blue suit.

I said, 'Ali?'

The Indian's eyes glowed a grin out of a bony face. 'Thass what my mudder calls me.'

'You bought the house over the road?'

'I bought a lotta houses.'

I said, 'What did you give for it? I'm interested.'

He looked me over, put a mug under the urn and squirted tea into it, walked round to a table, put the mug down, sat down on one side and pointed to the chair opposite. 'Drink some tea.'

I sat down. He chirped, 'You buy sell property?'

'Just now I'm buying.'

'Oh, I buying also.'

'Maybe you got something to sell?'

The high voice sing-songed, 'Could be. For quick money I sell.'

I pointed at the shop across the road, the one I wanted.

'That yours?'

He pointed at the row, and flashed white teeth again. 'Those five all mine.'

'What will you take for the shop?'

Smiling, he shook his head.

I said, 'What would you take for one of the others?'

He pointed. 'You see end one?' It was derelict, unoccupied. 'End one I sell.'

'How much?'

'Five hundred pound.'

'You're crazy. You can give that one to the wreckers. You'll never get a penny for it.'

'You come and see?'

We crossed the road and went over the house. He kept quiet, hung behind me smiling as I prowled about. The windows were smashed, the floorboards rotten, soaked ceilings had fallen in to expose their skeleton laths, great stains ate away the walls. A house like this, the council could make you spend a thousand pounds before a tenant set foot in it, if they enforced their regulations. On the other hand...When did the inspectors ever come near these houses? Marcia had told me. They could condemn them, for unfitness, for overcrowding. But if they did, the councils would have to put the people somewhere. Do you know how much a week it costs to keep a family in a public institution? I don't, but it's plenty. The destitute, the broken, the coloured, the dangerous, the unemployable swarm in these houses, in these streets. Even the respectable poor are afraid of them. Who wants them disturbed? Who wants them roaming the city for new shelter? No, the councils leave these houses alone. And I figured, for peanuts, for a hundred, I could make this house basically habitable. New windows, some new planking, a bit of plaster and cheap paper on the walls, a new water-closet—a hundred pounds would see me out. I could win that in one night at the track, once I had the house. Or Gus would stake me, with the house already in my possession as proof that I was going steady. It was bursting in my head like rockets, the excitement of treading these rotten boards. My house. My own. My stake in life. This wreck, this stinking ruin—it could be mine. I could get a whole tribe of immigrants in here, straight off the boat, paying me a pound a week each to kip on mattresses on the floor. My golden future.

The Indian chirruped, 'Well, Mister—?'

'Boas. I'll give you a hundred.'

He went off into a shrill parakeet laugh. 'Very funny. Very funny joke. George. Your name George?'

'Harry. Harryboy.'

This sent him off into a new squeaking fit. 'Harryboy. Ali-boy. Like brothers. Very funny. You my brother, Harryboy. Listen, Harryboy, I like you very much. For quick money, four hundred pounds.'

'For quick money, I'll do you a favour, one-fifty.'

We crossed back to the café. On the way he said, 'You got cash?'

'Cash.'

'Three hundred.'

We went into the café. I said, 'Two hundred. This is my limit.'

He was smiling, flashing his teeth, quacking with squeaky little laugh noises. 'And three hundred is my limit.'

'I'm not kidding, Ali.'

'Two-fifty?'

'Two hundred is my top.'

'Good, good,' he sang. 'Very good. Very good indeed.' He put his hand out, his face all grin. 'You got cash?'

'Yeh. I got cash. For your lawyer.'

'Why lawyer? I got deeds here. Wait.' He went into the back room and came out with a tin box. From the box he took out a sheaf of folded paper bundles. His high voice sang at me, 'Deeds for my property all in here. One, two, t'ree, four, five. You see? Deeds for your house here.' He tossed a packet on the table.

'Listen, Ali-boy. It's got to have a stamp on it. See? And a receipt. I want a receipt.'

He laughed like a joyful little boy. 'Very good, Harryboy. Very good. All right, I got a jolly good lawyer. We go to your lawyer or my lawyer?'

I always figure if a lawyer hasn't been disbarred I can deal with him, so I said, 'Yours will do.'

I was looking across at the three Africans. Still like graven images, they were brooding over the music of the dice rolling clickety-click on the marble table. The Indian was looking at me. He said, 'You like dose tings?'

'Nah.'

He laughed. 'You a doggy boy. Who is going to pay the lawyer?'

'We both pay the lawyer.'

He said, 'I tell you who pay the lawyer.' He put his hand out and without a word one of the Africans dropped the dice into it. 'You shoot crap?'

'I have done.' In Paris, when I was young, I used to shoot craps.

He said, 'The dice tell us who pay the lawyer.'

I looked at him. For three seconds I looked into his eyes and neither of us spoke. Then I reached out for the dice.

I won.

He kept looking at me and smiling. I kept looking at him. 'A gambler, Harryboy. Ali is also a gambler.'

'Sometimes I gamble.'

He said again, in the same, high, chiding voice, 'You are a gambler, Harryboy. Ali is also a gambler.'

'So?'

'Ask Ali's wife if he is a gambler. Aie, she cries. Harryboy, you are a gambler.'

My mouth was getting dry. 'I think you got a proposition.'

'My proposition is—' He drew it out playfully. 'You want a house without paying?'

'What do I put up?'

'You got cash? Two hundred?'

Another long three seconds. We were looking into each other's eyes like a pair of amateur hypnotists. Always in his, the smile. I said, 'I put up my two hundred against your deeds?'

He clicked the dice in his hand. 'Pretty music.'

The Africans had come over. They stood behind him and they were already looking at the table where the dice were going to fall. I didn't want to do this, but already in my gambler's mind there was no alternative.

So we shot craps, and his dice fell three and five, and I tipped the dice casually out of my hand, and got a natural.

I was a house-owner. At last.

'I told you,' Ali sang gaily. 'I said you would have a house without paying.'

I was a house-owner. All I had to do was go home.

'Oh,' Ali said merrily, 'I am a gambler. A terrible gambler. My poor wife. My poor children. A terrible, terrible gambler.' He threw another packet on the table. 'The same stakes?'

I looked at Ali. I looked at the Africans. I wondered, how did they know? Is there a mark on my forehead? What did I have to lose? Only winnings. If I lost the deeds, I still had my two hundred to buy them back. After this one I would walk out.

We rolled, and it took time for this one to come out, the ivories clicking again and again over the marble. Until Ali threw a seven. He pushed the second packet of deeds across to me.

I owned two houses. And now—have you ever gripped a rail charged with electricity? That was how it was going through me, like a shock, the old excitement, the old song inside my head, *don't be mad, don't walk out of a winning streak.*

And I won again, and Ali was gayer than ever.

And then I won again, and the deeds of four houses were stacked next to my hand.

And now, with my heart thumping, I was two men. One wanted the fifth house—the one I had come for in the first place. The other man was ready to go home.

Ali smiled and watched me in silence. The three Africans stood behind him. Their arms were folded and they were not looking at the table, but at me. It came to me how tall they were, tall and thin. Seven feet high they looked. They stood there as if they were in blankets with long spears. And it also came to me that they were between me and the door.

They stood between me and the door and they looked at me. No expression. They just looked.

Ali chuckled. He was waggling the last set of deeds in front of me. 'This you wanted all the time, eh? But for these I raise the stake. I put these against these—' he pointed at the other deeds—'and that.' He indicated my wallet, fat with two hundred pounds, on the table.

Did I have a choice? Supposing I tried to walk out now. They could have me carved and tossed over the back yard wall in ten seconds. If I was going to risk this, I might as well risk the stuff on the table.

On the other hand—I measured my distance to the window, and wondered if I could throw a chair through the plate glass to attract attention. Attention—in this street? This is not the age of miracles, and no police car came rolling by.

So we shot craps. I lost.

Ali took his deeds back. He took my money. The Africans just kept on looking at me. Ali saw me to the door, chuckling, 'Jolly good. Jolly good. Jolly good fellow.'

For ten minutes I had fulfilled one of my dreams. I had owned a row of houses. But I was me. Should I be surprised at how it ended?

He beamed at me from the door of his café. 'Good-a-bye, Harryboy.'

'So long, Ali-boy.'

Empty, the burden of possession lifted from me, I walked away.

*   *   *

Gregory said to his mother, 'It's not fair. I have to sleep by myself, and you and Daddy can cuddle each other all night.'

Evelyn said, 'Gregory!'

'Can I cuddle you when Daddy's dead?'

Vic laughed, but Evelyn said in a shocked tone, 'Gregory! How can you say such things?'

It was a few weeks after my epic game of craps. The Deaners had invited me to supper. This was ham, salad without any dressing, bread and butter and lemonade. I am not sneering. Hospitality, not food, is what matters. But poor Evelyn, for all her fanatical housework, was no good in the kitchen. Her family lived on simple fare. The sad thing was, she would not let Vic bring home a nice hot packet of fish and chips, which he had enjoyed as a regular treat in his single days. She thought it was 'common'.

Gregory had been allowed to stay up to have supper with the grown-ups as a special treat. He had behaved himself all day to earn this. He had laid the table for supper, putting out all the cutlery correctly, a very solemn task. He was always a good boy if you gave him any useful job to perform. I didn't think his parents made enough of this.

After supper his mother told him to go and wash before bed, and he trotted away. I remarked that he was a good boy. His mother said, 'For a wonder! I do wish I could get him into nursery school. I have him fourteen hours a day. He wears me out.'

We drank our coffee. The silence once Gregory had gone was so pleasant that none of us wanted to spoil it. There was a knock at the door. It was Siskin. His eyes looked three times as scared as usual. 'Please,' he said. 'Please come.'

I said, 'Where?'

'Miss Gosling. I can't make her talk to me. I don't know what's the matter. She didn't pay her rent today, I went to her room—'

Vic and I went up the stairs with Siskin talking at us from behind and Evelyn behind him. The door of Miss Gosling's room was open. The room was dark, with heavy plush curtains and it was crowded with old furniture like the cellar of a junk shop. The floor was dirty and littered with bonbon wrappers. The smell of unemptied slops was sickening. In a tall, wing-back armchair by the window sat Miss Ethel Gosling. Her head was tilted back and her hands lay on the arms of the chair.

I got to her first. Behind me Siskin was still gabbling. The old woman's breath came in snores. Her eyes were closed. Her face was red and all the skin had dropped. Her body was like a sack in the chair.

I said, 'She's had a stroke.'

From behind us came a high, clear voice. 'She's the one who wouldn't give me any sweets.'

Gregory was in the room. Stampeding up past the bathroom, we had forgotten about him. He was looking at Miss Gosling with a calm, thoughtful gaze, as if he was in a museum. His mother muttered, 'Oh, my God,' ran to him, picked him up and hurried him downstairs.

I went to ring for the ambulance. When I came back, I looked into the Deaners' living-room. Evelyn sat there rocking Gregory on her lap. She jerked her head upwards to indicate that Vic was still upstairs, and went on crooning to Gregory, 'Let me tell you a story. Let Mummy tell you a nice story.'

Gregory said, 'She is deaded, isn't she?'

'No, dear. I told you. She is only ill.'

'She is deaded. God punished her because she wouldn't give me any sweets.'

'No, dear. The men are coming to take her to the hospital, and a nice doctor will make her better.'

Gregory said, 'The men will put her in a hole. With a stone on top. All the deads are in the churchyard. I ride my bike on top of them.'

'Don't talk about it, darling. Listen to Mummy's nice story.'

'I won't be very happy when I'm dead,' Gregory said. 'I won't be able to eat chocolate and I shall be just like the pavement.'

'Poor darling,' she murmured, hugging him to her, 'it's all too much for him.'

Was it, just! I will back a child for a good practical view of life and death any day. I had heard Gregory, after seeing the rows of corpses covered by blankets in a train disaster on the television news bulletin, say, 'Mummy, will they be able to mend the train?' And one evening we were looking at a film of a famine in India, and his daddy said that these were poor people who hadn't got enough to eat. Gregory said anxiously, 'You won't give them any of our food, Daddy?' Mankind naked—that is a child.

As I went out to see if the ambulance was coming, Gregory was saying, 'Can I go up and look at her again? Please Mummy, let me have another look.'

*   *   *

Vic and I came out of the Metropolitan Hospital at eleven o'clock that night. The old lady had died a half-hour earlier. It was dark and cool. We walked with pleasure, listening to the sound of our shoes on the pavement in the night silence.

'Well,' Vic said, 'so that's how they go.'

'That's how they go.'

'Makes you wonder if it's all worth while.'

'What?'

'Life.'

I like the London streets at night when they are empty. The shops were lit and their neon signs were on, the wide Kingsland Road ran away from us without a human being in sight, and traffic lights winked in three colours uselessly. Night is when you can stretch your legs, walk fast, think. For Vic, evidently, it was a time to talk. He said, 'What do you think?'

'Me?'

'About life?'

'You know the story of the two Jews? One of them said, "What's the matter, don't you want to know how my health is?" The other one said, "Well, how is your health?" The first one said, "Don't ask me."'

Vic chewed on this one for a few seconds. 'Anyway,' he said, 'you enjoy it.'

'Enjoy what?'

'Life.'

We crossed a road. He said, 'We're here today, gone tomorrow. That's the thing to do, enjoy it.'

'Yes.'

He said, 'I do like talking to you. I don't seem to be able to talk to other people. Isn't it a lovely night?'

'Yeh.'

'Shame about the old lady.'

'Yeh.'

He said, 'You've got the right idea. Enjoy life. You make it quickly and you spend it quickly.'

'Quickly is right.'

'God, I wish I knew how to do it quickly.'

'You'll be all right. Couple of years' time, you'll be qualified.'

'I'll be lucky if I'm making money in five years. Five years! We can all be dead by then.'

'Five years, you'll have everything.'

'Why aren't I the kind that can have it now? Like you. I sit there at my books every night. I can hear people walking down the street, laughing, cars whooshing past. Life is outside. I'm stuck with my books. What for? I can drop dead before I get the benefit.'

'You'll be all right.'

'When I think of you,' he said. 'You walked round that dog track as if you owned the place. My goodness, all you do is go there and collect your money.'

'Yeh,' I said. 'That's all I have to do.'

'I wish I had your luck,' he said. 'It's just like going to the bank for you.'

'Well,' I said. 'It's luck.'

'You've got the courage,' he said. 'That's why. You deserve the luck, you do. Because you've got the courage.'

'It takes nerve,' I said.

'Yes,' he said, 'that's just the word. That's just what it takes. Nerve.'

*　　　　*　　　　*

Well, my story runs from the start of one year to the start of the next, and at this point the chain of events, one touching off another, gets more rapid and violent.

I ask myself, looking back, who started it? Who gave the first push? Was it me, boasting to Vic about money and not seeing what I was doing? Was it the Almighty, when he killed Miss Ethel with a clot of blood on the brain? In the affairs of people, where can you find a beginning? If the blame for what finally happened was human, we could as well lay it at the feet of poor old Siskin, when he let the room which had once been occupied by the late Miss Gosling.

He let it to a coloured couple. 'Who else,' he said to me, 'would give three pounds a week for that room?'

They had the aristocratic name of de Souza, and they were West Indians. They were young, and they were nice people. The wife was too broad in the bosom and the cheekbones for my taste, but she was all good nature. The husband was tall, relaxed, with the skin of a bronze sculpture and handsome like Harry Belafonte. He was a warehouseman in the ironmongery line.

I got on all right with them. Siskin had his troubles with them, about which I will tell you later, but he had to admit they were, as he said, 'lovely people'. Gregory seemed to like them. He came up and stood on the landing and inspected them, ate whatever titbit Milly de Souza gave him (and she was a good cook) and trotted downstairs contented. Vic was a man too short of friends to rebuff this friendly couple, and I thought he was going to get on good terms with them. The trouble was Evelyn.

She went mad because there were coloured people in the house.

The first time Vic came up, after they had moved in, I was sitting on the top of my three steps eating a plate of bananas fried in rum that Milly de Souza had passed to me. I should explain that there is a skylight in the ceiling of this top landing. Joe, the husband, was the first inhabitant of the house since Noah to realise that this skylight could let in fresh air. So he had put up a ladder, fixed a pulley and cord that would open and close the skylight from below, and washed the dirt of years off the panes. As a result, we had a cool and light landing on these early summer evenings, on which the de Souzas not only cooked, but ate, so that Milly could hand her specialities straight from the stove to the table. I said no thank you to their invitation to supper which, like sensible people, they gave easily but didn't push, but I had their dessert with them, and my belly decided that these were good neighbours.

Vic came up for a talk, and soon he was sitting next to me, eating his portion of fried bananas and chatting with the de Souzas.

Then Evelyn called up, 'Vic!'

He yelled down, 'I'm up here with Harry, dear.'

She was standing in the ground-floor hall. She shouted, as if she was calling her child downstairs, 'Vic, I want you.'

He answered, 'I won't be long.'

And then she shrieked, 'Vic, come down!'

Shrieked is the only word. It sounded like a shriek from a madhouse. The de Souzas went on eating just a little too deliberately. Vic flushed and he got up as another, 'Vic, do you hear me!' rang in the hall below.

He went downstairs. I heard him and Evelyn go into the bedroom, and from the bang of the door I knew that there was trouble.

CHAPTER TWELVE

When Evelyn went about the house or into the street there was nothing changed in her manner except for an extra coldness and wariness. She said 'good morning' and 'good evening' to the de Souzas.

But inside her flat she was a fury. She lived in a continual quivering silence out of which she darted, without warning, spurts of shrill protest and abuse at her husband. She was like a hissing snake in her kitchen.

I was down there one evening, while he was putting his homework away. By now he had attached himself to me like the ivy on the old garden wall. The kid was in bed. The television, for a change, was switched off. Evelyn was looking at the *Daily Mirror*.

'It's ridiculous,' she said. 'Look at these hats.' She showed us the photograph. 'Can you imagine me wearing one? I think they must design these hats for exhibitionists.'

Then, at once, she smashed her hands together with the newspaper in them, and her face twisted, and she said, 'It's the last straw. It's really the last straw.'

She wasn't speaking naturally. She was fighting for breath. 'How he could do a thing like that?—let those people into the house—I can't understand it. I really can't. You know'—she turned to me—'there's only one water-closet in this house.'

That was how these spasms of hate came to her, like attacks. She turned her bitter face upon Vic. 'It really is the last straw. I came here. I didn't complain. I put up with this house. This street. You said it wouldn't be for long. Didn't you? Don't deny it. You said we wouldn't be here for long. I've kept our child away from all these roughs. And now look what happens. In this house. Inside this house. Well? Well? What do you expect me to do now? Put up with it? I'm asking you, Victor. Do you expect me to put up with it?'

He said, 'They don't do us any harm. We never see or hear them.'

'You don't. You're at work all day. I'm at home. I'm at home with our child all day. Suppose that man came home early. Eh? Have you thought of that? Have you given a thought to that? We never see or hear them, do we? With the street door open. Did you know that? We live in a house with the street door open, now. Like a slum. All their friends trampling in and out. The whole brigade.' She laughed. 'The whole Caribbean brigade. That's what we have to live with now.'

Vic said, 'Evelyn, you mustn't be prejudiced.'

'Don't tell me I'm prejudiced. Please don't tell me now that I'm prejudiced. I know there are good and bad. Thank you, I know that. I'm not illiterate. Some of them are good enough for Royalty to shake hands with. Look at these Indian rajahs. All right, and do you know what this one is? A labourer. He comes home filthy. Filthy. What do you think I am—one of these colour bar people? That's how you try and change the subject. This man is a labourer. This is the house we have to bring our child up in. Well?'

'Well?' he said. 'What can I do?'

'Get us out of here, that's what you can do. Get some money. Use your brains. For God's sake, you've got brains, haven't you? It's a poor look-out for us if you haven't.'

'Evelyn, be patient. I've got to wait for my exams.'

'Thank you. Two more years. Two more years in a slum street. I've worked my fingers to the bone getting a nice home together. I might as well put a match to the whole lot. I've worked for nothing. For nothing. It's not enough there's all colours in the street, we've got them in the house now.'

He said, 'I'm going out now.'

'Do. With your friend,' she said, speaking as if I was black, too, 'and while you're out, you'd better think of some ways and means of finding us a decent home. I come from a good class family, and I'm not going to stay in a slum for you or anyone.'

We went out, and Vic told me miserably that he was getting this every night, more and more hysterical, and he was so worried that he was thinking of trying to get her to see a doctor about her nerves.

*　　　　　*　　　　　*

Siskin had his troubles with them, too. There was nothing wrong with them except that they were happy people, and they had come into a house in which previously even the squeak of a mouse had passed for a loud and unseemly disturbance.

They did the room out at their own expense. Joe de Souza was a great handyman. Siskin, watching the bright wallpaper go up with no charge to him, was duly appreciative. They brought in nice furniture, which they had got on weekly payments. And they put a washing machine in the bathroom, which they invited us all to use as if it was our own. Evelyn, whose code squeezed a sort of strangled civility out of her, managed a thin-lipped 'thank you' to this, though she never touched the thing.

The trouble was, they had friends. They went to church every Sunday morning, splendidly dressed, and after the service there clumped into the house with them a crowd of big men and stout, smiling women whose laughter resounded through the house above the clatter of their teacups. During the week Milly de Souza left the street door open so that her women friends could use her washing-machine, and all the afternoon I could hear them tramping up and down the stairs.

Siskin, poor Siskin, was worse than Evelyn. He was demented with fright. He plucked up courage, and stopped Joe de Souza in the hall one day, and mumbled, 'Please, the door. You won't leave it open? Burglars could come in.'

'Gee!' The concern in Joe's face was tragic. 'I'm sorry, Mr Siskin. The last thing I wanted to do was worry you.'

The next morning he took a big box of chocolates down to the basement for that poor old crow, Siskin's wife.

And two days later, Siskin heard the sound of a key in the lock, and a strange woman walked in. A little later, another key and another woman. And another a half-hour later. It turned out that Joe, in his anxiety to reassure Mr Siskin, had had a dozen street-door keys cut and had given them out among his friends.

So once again Siskin trembled, and screwed himself up for days, and at last accosted Joe, and mumbled, 'Mr de Souza, please, you don't mind. All these keys? I don't like strangers should have keys. Your friends I'm not saying nothing against. But a key gets lost, a burglar can come in and break my head. All night I can't sleep.'

So poor Joe collected in the keys and gave them to Siskin, with a cake his wife had baked. And that day there was a thunder of the door-knocker, and Milly came down to open the door to a friend. And soon after, the knocker banged again, and Milly came down again. And all day long the house shook to the sound of the door-knocker, and Siskin wept.

At last he spoke, this time to me, and begged me to intercede, and I said to de Souza, 'Joe, you're living in a house of the dead. I don't know what to advise you.'

Joe took it with a big, good-humoured grin, and went down to apologise with a huge and beautiful bunch of flowers such as had never been seen in that stinking cellar before.

From that time on, all was quiet. On other front doorsteps coloured boys played the guitar while their friends gathered round and sang. In other back yards steel band parties were held far into the night. On Sunday mornings the churchgoers went back to other houses for tea, and I could hear their laughter passing in the street. But in our house, all was quiet. The de Souzas sat unvisited and went out for their social pleasures. As Joe said to me, 'We only try to please.'

He pleased Siskin. The old man hobbled about, muttering, 'Lovely people. A mensch. A gentleman. Three pounds a week and never late a day.'

But nothing he did could please Evelyn. After a couple of weeks she went down to see Siskin—she had tried to make Vic do it, but for the first time in their life as far as I knew he had stood up to her and refused—and she demanded that he get rid of the de Souzas. She said, 'Either they go or we go. Well, Mr Siskin. Which is it to be? Do you want to lose respectable tenants?'

The old man rocked himself and said, 'They are nice people. What can I do? I can't insult them. How can I get rid of them? Every Friday come six o'clock the husband pays the rent. What can I do?'

'All right,' said Evelyn. 'If they don't go, we will. You can expect my notice, Mr Siskin. Just as soon as I find somewhere to go.'

She went upstairs, to tell Vic, I suppose, that she had burned their boats behind them.

*   *   *

Milly said to me, 'Why don't she like us?'

I was too busy polishing my plate to answer. It was a Saturday. They had called me down to help them dispose of a chicken in chilli sauce.

Joe said, 'I tell you why, Mill. We got too much life. We are not liked because we have too much life in us.'

Through a mouthful I said, 'Maybe.'

'You,' Joe said, 'you got nothing against us, Harry. I tell you why. You got plenty of life, too. I seen you eat.'

'Eat?'

'Yeh. I watched you eat that chicken. Boy, the way you tore that wing off, and crunched that bone, and sucked the marrow out, and wiped your plate. You sure made a meal of it.'

'So?'

'Listen, that's how I like to see a man eat. But not her. Not that lady downstairs.'

'She doesn't like me so much either.'

'Go on, man, you're the best of pals with them.'

'In a friendly way she hates me, too.'

He thought over this for a moment, and then said, 'Sure. Sure, I get it.'

'You see,' I said, 'the way we eat, that way we live. You and me, Joe, we mop the plate dry. We suck the last gob of marrow. We lick our fingers. From our fathers and our grandfathers we know hunger, and we value food. In our blood we know an axe can fall on us at any second. So we live. We live.'

'Sure,' Joe said.

Sure, I nearly added, and these haters of life, they can even murder babies. Because that moment brought back to me, like a twitch of pain in the head, my fear that a little son of mine might have been packed into a dark, suffocating, sealed truck for five days and nights and sent to the furnaces.

*   *   *

Evelyn was stuck with her own ultimatum. Vic had to go to work every day, and anyhow, he was in no hurry to move. So she had to study the 'accommodation vacant' columns in the North London papers and tramp the streets in search of a new flat. It's hard to think of a more nerve-racking task than house-hunting for people who are tired, desperate and short of money. She started with the more pleasant suburbs along the Green Belt, the places she dreamed of moving to, but the rents were way above her reach. She came down through the shabbier, jerry-built suburbs on the marshes of the River

Lea, and in a few weeks she was back in Hackney, trudging through streets as crowded and grubby as our own. Too many people are chasing too few homes. Evelyn just didn't have enough money to compete. She got nowhere, and it drove her even more crazy, and she rubbed it off on Vic, at whom I could hear her screaming in the evenings, blaming him for their lack of money. Of course, little Gregory was having to live with all this.

At first she yanked him around with her, but the strain, on top of the strain of searching, was too much for her. She could only occasionally leave him with Vic's mother. The sick old woman doted on the child but couldn't cope with him for more than an hour or two. So the job came back to Harryboy Boas.

I didn't mind. I was in a mood to enjoy the summer afternoons. I had plenty of money. A gambler's life is up and down, and for me this was an up period at the tracks.

Gregory took to imitating me. He would stand on the landing and call to me, using the voice in which I called to him, 'Come on, feller!' He dropped a sweet in the gutter, and he stood over it with his head cocked to one side and his arms akimbo, and he said in my voice, 'Such is my form.' One day his mother told him off and he yakked back, 'Ah, you're meshuggah!'

She pressed her lips together, and with one of those so-subtle side-glances at me she said, 'Gregory! Where do you get these awful expressions?'

She hated him imitating me. But I exulted.

*   *   *

I have a conscience. I tried to put Vic wise to what was happening. What substitute is there for a child's own parents? But Vic, poor Vic, had too much love in his heart for the child, he could not see any danger, only pleasure for his kid. I urged him to keep a half-day free every weekend for Gregory. I pointed out that London was full of free marvels for a child, and a child should share them, and the memory of them, with his father. At least, I said, let us take him together.

But, 'You take him,' he said, for the most part. 'If you don't mind, that is. I do want him to enjoy himself. I must get on with my study. After all, I am doing it for him.'

So I took Gregory on the Underground Railway, which he had never seen before, and he went mad riding up and down the moving staircases.

I took him on boat trips down the river and he climbed all over on the old sailing ship down at Greenwich, playing at sailors. I took him to see the guns, the suits of armour and the Beefeaters at the Tower of London. We fed the deer and the ducks in the parks. The Science Museum was a paradise for him, with its press-button models in glass cases and its miniature coal mine to roam through. I kept him out late one evening to show him that firework display of coloured lights in Piccadilly Circus. Thank goodness his parents had no idea what he ate in the course of one afternoon with me, ice creams, candy bars and hamburgers one on top of another. Swings, seesaws and roundabouts in the playgrounds. Popeye cartoons at the newsreel cinema.

It reached the point where, even when Vic did make free time for himself, the kid was reluctant to go out with him.

*   *   *

The three of us were on one of our Sunday morning walks. Vic and I were talking about books—we were both at that time searching out psychological thrillers at the library, the kind the Americans do well, Vera Caspary, Patricia Highsmith and so on, and recommending them to each other. Gregory was roaming on ahead.

Round the corner came an Alsatian. Now, Gregory in the normal way had no fear of dogs. But this animal was huge. Even to me it seemed the size of a small pony. And it was trotting fast, with its head down, and it came round the corner suddenly, right on top of the child.

He turned, let out a howl and flew back towards us. Vic called out to him not to worry, but the child was struck with terror. He did not look round. His feet twinkled under him and he ran with a long howl, his arms outstretched.

Vic squatted down to receive him, and held out his arms.

But the child flew past him like a little fleeing rabbit, and I had myself to squat before he cannoned into my knees, and he flung himself against me, his arms round my neck, sobbing. I had to put my arms round him, and I had to murmur comfort in his ears.

I looked over his shoulder, as I stroked him, at his father. His father looked at me. At last Vic had understood. His face was piteous.

CHAPTER THIRTEEN

I have a conscience. To come between a child and his parents, no thank you, this is not my wish. I decided that I would get hold of Vic the next day and give him a good talking-to.

But something happened to forestall me. Next morning Vic called me from downstairs. I went down. He said to me, 'Gregory's gone all funny.'

I went into the bedroom with him. Evelyn sat on the edge of the bed in her dressing-gown. Gregory lay in her arms. His face was flushed and his breathing was awful, as if there was a whistle in his throat.

Evelyn didn't speak. She just rocked him and looked at me in her brooding, hostile way. Vic said, 'Feel his skin.'

I laid my hand on the child's forehead. It was like a furnace, and dry.

Vic said, 'He woke us up at five o'clock. He was sick. He didn't bring up any food, just water. He was sick again at seven. I can't understand, he doesn't make any noise, it's not like him.'

This was the strangest thing in that room, the silence. Gregory lay in his mother's arms, and all he did when I came in was to open his eyes and look at me dully, his eyes following me like those of an animal in pain. He could have been dumb, there was not a whimper. Then he closed his eyes again with a terrible aged weariness.

Vic said, 'I can't go to work and leave him like this. I went out just after eight and phoned the health service doctor. His wife wouldn't call him. She said he was having breakfast. She took a message.'

Evelyn said, 'Go round to the doctor.'

Vic said, 'He doesn't go to his surgery till nine.'

Her voice was low and like a knife, 'Go to his house. Bring him here.'

I said, 'I'll go.'

She said, 'I've got a husband.'

She and I looked at each other. She kept rocking the child all the time.

Vic said, 'I'll ring him once more, first.'

He went out. Evelyn, always with that gleam of hate in her eyes, murmured to me, 'Get some water. Take the chill off it.'

I went to the kitchen for water. I came back with the cup. She took it from me. Gregory was moaning very softly. His skin was fiery red, and the dry heat burned through him. His breathing screeched, and his lips were cracked with dryness. The name of an illness was already running through my mind. I did not speak it. She wetted the child's lips.

Vic came back. He said to me, in the hall, 'I spoke to the doctor. He'll call in before surgery.' He grasped my arm. 'It could be polio.'

This was the word in my mind, but I said, 'Nah. Wait for the doctor.'

'I keep thinking, polio. I know I shouldn't talk about it, but you do hear of these cases. You can't help thinking, can you?'

'What are you talking about out there?' It was Evelyn's voice, cold and bitter.

Vic would not go to work. He made tea, and roamed about the flat. Evelyn put the child to bed and sat by the bedside, watchful and silent.

The doctor came an hour later. He walked in, examined the half-conscious child in a deft, quick, rough way, said, 'He'll be all right,' wrote a prescription, told Vic to take it to the chemist's and picked up his bag. He found Evelyn in his path. Her eyes were blazing. She said, 'You can't walk out like this.'

'He'll be all right,' the doctor said wearily. 'It's just a bronchial spasm. Children get these high temperatures, and it passes. Just keep him in bed.' She did not move, and he said, smiling, 'What did you think it was? Polio?'

She lingered for a second, then stepped out of his path, and he went out. Vic hovered. He said, 'I don't like to leave him like this.'

She said, 'Go to work.'

'But I'm—Gregory—the chemist's.'

'Harry will get the prescription. Go to work.'

He went. I got the prescription from the chemist, a bottle of small white pills. She forced one into the child's mouth. His breathing kept a steady rhythm. She said to me, 'He's going off to sleep. I shall be all right.'

I stood wondering if I ought to keep her company. She smiled ironically. 'I can cope. Don't worry.'

I left her. Towards midday I looked in again. The child was asleep. She sat at the bedside exactly as I had left her. I told her to get something to eat. She said curtly, 'I'm all right.' I made some tea for her. She took it without thanks.

Late in the afternoon I looked in again. She still sat there. Gregory was still sleeping.

I went out for the evening papers, stayed chatting with the boys in the barber's shop for a while, and came back to the house. Evelyn called me from the bedroom door. She said, 'Look at him.'

Gregory was sitting on the bedroom floor playing with his toys. At his side was a plate of toast smeared with Marmite, and he was just in the act of tearing at a slice with his teeth like a hungry little beast.

He saw me and uttered his usual demand, in his usual loud voice, 'Play with me.'

Evelyn said, 'He woke up half-an-hour ago and he was perfectly normal. You'd never believe there'd been anything wrong with him.'

Another peremptory yell from him. 'Harryboy, I said play with me.'

Evelyn said, 'Play with your toys. Leave Harryboy alone.'

Astonishingly, he said, in a meek voice, 'Yes, Mummy,' and went back to his toys and toast.

Shutting the door on him, Evelyn said to me, 'Don't look so surprised. He's Mummy's boy today. He'll be raising hell again tomorrow. Telling me I'm wicked. I've got some tea on, in the kitchen.'

I went into the other room with her. She said, 'When he's ill, he wants his mummy to cuddle him.'

'Maybe that's the only time she does.'

'It's marvellous. Everyone who hasn't got a baby knows all about bringing them up. Of course, I know I'm a bad mother. I've seen you looking at me sometimes when I had to speak to him sharply or punish him. You're the expert, I'm only the mother, I don't know anything.'

'I mind my own business, Evelyn.'

'That's a laugh. The way you watch sometimes. He plays hell, I try to cope, and you stand there watching as if I was the criminal. Of course, you think you're the cat's whiskers, don't you? He eats out of your hand, so you think you can manage him and his parents can't. Just because he knows how to get round you. Well, let me tell you, he's got round a lot of other people, too. His grandparents, for one thing. He's God's little angel to them. He can do no wrong. It was the same with the neighbours where we used to live. If I smacked him he was the poor injured little innocent.'

I said something about everyone sympathising with a parent's difficulties, and sipped my tea.

'Oh, no,' she said, 'tell the truth. You think I'm wicked. You think I'm a bad mother. Well, I'd like to see you do the work I do, and feel as tired as I do, and keep your temper. I'm tired, I'm tired right through. I could just lie down and sleep for a week. All I do is work. I never get a moment. You try that, and then see if you can keep your temper when he gets on your nerves. It's all right for you. You and his grandparents. You're always on his side. He knows that. That's why he plays up to you. But we have to do the dirty work. We're his parents. We have to teach him that there are certain things he mustn't do. And he doesn't like that. So he kicks and screams with us, and he's the misunderstood little darling to everyone else.'

I said, 'I know.'

'I don't think you do. I'm the only one that knows. The bad mother. My God, you go in the other room and look at him. He's a bonny child, isn't he? Well, I made him like that. I did. You should have seen him when he was born. A poor wizened little mite. Pinched little face. Underweight. I had to give him three-hour feeds for the first couple of months. First one at six in the morning, last one at midnight. And each feed took an hour. He hadn't even got the strength to suck. I just had to keep him on the breast and be patient. I didn't have half a night's sleep before he was eighteen months old. There was his teething and his vaccination and his poor little sore bottom, it was red raw, I used to listen to this poor little bundle whimpering with misery every night, it broke my heart, do you think I begrudged staying up all night to comfort him? Till that child was three I put the food into him spoon by spoon. Have you seen how I feed him, even now? We're not big eaters, either Vic or me. For one thing we can't afford to be on Vic's wages. Do you know what I give that child every day? Steaks. He eats steaks like a man. He can eat a half-a-pound of meat in a day. That's what's put the flesh on him. And it costs money. More than we can afford. Go and have a look at his clothes. Prince Charles isn't dressed better than my child. And his toys. Who do you think saves up so that he can have all these things? Only his bad mother. I work miracles with Vic's wages. It's all for the child.'

I said, 'I know, Evelyn. I know.'

'You'll never know. Why don't you get married and have one of your own? I've done my very best for that child. I've given him all the love he could want. I've scraped pennies for him. And all he does is just trample on me.'

'You can't expect gratitude from a child.'

'I never said gratitude. But a little love sometimes. A little gentleness. Sometimes he seems to just want deliberately to wear me out. He sees me working for him all the time. Can't he see how tired I am? He makes a noise, and he sees it upsets me, so he purposely goes on making it all the morning. He can keep it up for hours and hours. If I'm tired, and I just want to rest, he'll pounce on me like an animal. He has no mercy. No mercy at all. You don't know how rude he can get sometimes, and how silly.'

'It's a fight, Evelyn. A child fights for life. He fights for his own wants. You're right, he has no mercy.'

'All right. I've read these child psychologies as well. But a person only has so much endurance. I'm only human. I can't help remembering sometimes that I was once a free person and not the slave of a little wild animal.' She laughed wryly. 'You know, his trouble was, he came too soon.'

She brought in hot water and gave us fresh tea. 'I had a lovely job,' she said. 'I was in a business office. Honestly, I just enjoyed every day of it. We used to have so many laughs, and I used to love looking round the shops in the lunch hour. I was never one of those who hated going to work. Even after I was married. It made me feel free, going out every morning, and having the ride on the bus. It was easy, too, compared with housework. I never felt tired in those days. And I earned jolly good money. Vic and I could afford our little pleasures then. We were going to put five pounds a week away in the post office. We had it all worked out. In three years we'd have enough to put down a deposit on a house. Then we'd start a family.' Another laugh. 'But unfortunately our family came three years too soon. So—no job for me. No savings. No house. We pinch and scrape and we live in a dirty street with blacks in the house.'

I kept quiet and she said, 'I wouldn't complain. I wouldn't complain. If only I could feel he was mine, my baby. But he just goes his own way. I'm just someone he takes for granted, to wait on him twenty-four hours a day. That's my life. Do you know what he said to me? He said, "Mummy, you've got to love me, haven't you, because I'm your little boy?" You see, it's not only food, and toys, and money for sweets, he even wants kisses, he wants love. But what about me? Honestly, I feel sometimes as if I've given birth to—oh, I don't know what—a parasite, yes, that's the word. He clings to me, and sucks the blood out of me, and grows and grows. And when he's finished, he'll just walk away. And get married, I suppose.'

'Yes,' I said. 'And have babies.'

'Yes,' she said. 'And have babies. Oh it's all a big laugh.'

*   *   *

Well, there are two sides to every story, and that was Evelyn's.

We stopped talking.

I should have got up, but I stayed in my chair just too long for the movement to appear natural, and the silence became uncomfortable. She was sitting across the corner of the kitchen table looking at me with an odd fixity.

I stood up. She said, 'Are you strong?'

I said, 'Why?'

She got up, turned to the dresser, opened a drawer and rummaged in it. She held something out to me. I took it.

It was a tube of iron with a slit in the top, and it rattled. I said, 'It's a moneybox.'

'It's iron,' she said. 'It's a very old one. It's in two parts. Can you unscrew it for me?'

I looked at it. There was a hairline where the two parts met, and the thread was obviously on a flange that fitted inside, for there was nowhere to insert a knife to loosen it. I tried it and of course it was fast.

She said, 'It's very old. It's rusted solid.' I tried, then tried again, then took a proper grip on it, and tried with everything I had. It felt as solid as if it was welded. I wondered if the thread had warped and jammed inside. The thing annoyed me. I took a fresh grip and increased my leverage, more and more, till I could feel every muscle in me, legs, body, arms, clenched like iron behind the effort of my hands. My face was hot and I knew it must be getting redder, and I could feel the veins stand out on my temples and the ache of my teeth biting together hard. She had sat down again, with one hand limp on the table, and she was looking at me impassively. I felt as if I had been doing it a very long time, and I tried not to relax all the strength I had poured into my two hands turning against each other, and I tried not to make noises of strain in my throat.

Then I felt it start to give, and I forced more strength into my hands, and then it gave way, the threads squeaked, and I felt the two parts turn easily against each other. I had it open, and I could breathe, and the first time I did so my lungs hurt for a second. There were weals on my hands. I emptied the box, and about a dozen old farthings rolled out across the table. I said, 'There y'are, I've made you rich.'

She said, 'I've had it for years. Every time a workman came into the house I asked him to have a try.'

I said, 'It's a knack.'

'My husband couldn't have done that to save his life.'

'It's just the grip.'

'Is it?'

I said, 'I'd better go up and wash this rust off. I'm glad the kid's all right.'

She sat and watched me go, her eyes as brooding and hostile, it seemed, as before we had talked.

*   *   *

My great lecture to Vic was put off till the next day, a Saturday. But as it turned out, he was the one that gave the lecture.

An hour after lunch, just as I was waking up from my afternoon nap, I heard Gregory stampeding up the stairs and shouting, 'Harryboy! Harryboy!'

The door of my room hurtled open—this was how he made his entries— and there he stood. Slung from its strap over his shoulders was a leather school satchel. He shone with joy. 'Look, Harryboy. Look what my daddy bought me! My daddy bought me a shassel. My daddy bought me a big boy's shassel for when I start school!'

I said, 'Well, you are a big boy.'

'I will be five in three months, and after that I will go to school. My daddy is downstairs. Do you want to come and see my daddy?'

I went downstairs with him. I took the satchel to be a thankoffering, one of those things parents buy in the first flush of relief when their child has escaped some danger. Vic met me in the hall. He was beaming with happiness. 'Seems to be a success,' he said.

The kid stormed upstairs again to show his new satchel to the de Souzas. At the top of his voice he was singing one of those weird, wordless, endless, tuneless children's songs.

Vic said, 'You know you were saying I ought to go out with him more? Well, I've decided you were right. See him with that satchel? Like a dog with two tails. I mean, he's at the age when I ought to be teaching him things. I ought to be taking him to the ponds at Epping to catch tadpoles. And boxing with him. And I'm going to get him used to the alphabet, you know, just recognising letters. I mean, he'll be going to school in another term. I shall find the time for him at weekends, even if I have to work later at nights. After all, he needs me.'

Which was my lecture, given back to me on a plate. Vic said, 'I shall make a real start when we go on holiday.' He had two weeks in July. 'We're booking for Herne Bay. I shan't tell Gregory till we get confirmation from the boarding-house. I don't want to risk disappointing him.'

I said, 'How are you off for money? I could lend you.'

He answered me with a stiff dignity. 'We've got the money, thank you. Evelyn saves, you know. She puts by ten shillings a week. She's a wonderful manager.'

Upstairs we could hear Gregory's loud, jubilant boasting, and more softly the warm voices of the de Souzas.

*　　　　*　　　　*

Evelyn came out into the hall. She said, 'Where is he?' Vic pointed upstairs, where Gregory's voice resounded. She moved to the foot of the stairs, to shout up. Vic put his hand on her arm. 'Let him enjoy himself.'

'With them?'

'He won't come to any harm.'

'I want him downstairs.'

'Evelyn, if you call him downstairs he'll want explanations.'

'Why? I want him downstairs, that's all.'

'You can't just keep calling him down. He's too sharp. He'll understand you don't want him to talk to them.'

'Why shouldn't he understand?'

'He'll connect it with their colour.'

'Who said anything about colour? He knows very well by now I don't want him to mix with rough people.'

'I don't want you to give him any wrong ideas.'

'I know how to bring my own child up.' This was the old Evelyn again, hard, sharp, hysteria quivering under the skin of her face.

'He'll catch on that it's their colour,' Vic said. 'Do you want him frightened again? You know how easily he gets frightened. Do you want to have to stay up nights with him again?'

He turned to me. 'He's frightened of shadows,' he said. 'It's funny, he'll fight anyone, the bigger the better, but he gets terrified by so many strange things. We took him to a children's party once, and he screamed with terror when they put a handkerchief on his eyes for Blind Man's Buff. For nights afterwards he used to wake up and cry and Evelyn had to sit nursing him for hours.'

Evelyn said, 'All right.' She made a little defeated grimace with her lips and turned away. Then the craziness leaped in her voice again. 'God knows what they'll give him to eat up there. Do you know what they eat, those people? Tinned cat's meat. I've seen them buying it in the grocer's.'

Vic waited till the door had closed on her. 'I'm worried about her,' he said. 'She just keeps getting worse. She just won't stop. I try to tell her, we haven't got the money to move, but you can't argue with her. If only we had something for key-money. You can get flats if you can afford to bribe the landlord.'

'All right, I don't want to hurt your feelings, but if Evelyn finds a place, I can lend you the money. Why not? Who does it hurt?'

'You don't understand, it's being a failure—I'm supposed to be the breadwinner. Why can't I solve our own problems? Evelyn hates borrowing. She's making herself ill. Sometimes I feel it's all making me ill, too. I shall have to think of something—'

*   *   *

From now on Gregory wouldn't go anywhere without his satchel. 'He put it on over his pyjamas the first night when he went to bed,' Vic said reverently, 'only now we've persuaded him to put it next to his bed where he can see it when he opens his eyes.' It was a tremendous symbol to the kid. Wearing it, he marched about like a little Mussolini.

He came up to see me more than ever. As the summer days got longer, in July, he went to bed later, and although he and his daddy now went off on their own on Sundays, he started a habit of rushing up to see me in the evenings, before his bed-time, just when I was changing to go out.

This was a bit of a nuisance. In fact, I must now confess, the kid was becoming at times a nuisance in my life. You must know how it happens with adults. You have a friend. You're always glad to see him. One day you realise that you dread his ring at the doorbell. He's a nice fellow, but you wish he'd stop haunting you. And with women, at a certain point with a woman you get to feel the same way.

So now the kid started getting into my hair. I was in another of my long reading spells. I had got on to the three big Theodore Dreiser novels about Frank Cowperwood, the Philadelphia financier, and I was all set to go right through them. But how could I read when the kid kept bursting into my room? If I wanted to go for an evening mooch in the streets, he would be waiting for me in the hall.

I tried to reason with him, but I came up against a granite selfishness. He would never take 'no'. What he wanted at that moment was all that mattered. I had been a good friend to him. I would plead, 'Not now, son. I want to read. Let me read for an hour, and then you can come up.' Or I would promise, 'Tomorrow, Gregory.' No use, he would keep up his remorseless chant. 'Play with me. Play with me. Play with me. Play with me.' Or, 'Come out with me. Come out with me. Come out with me.'

Sometimes he looked a different child to me. His face puckered ugly and sulky and all I could see standing in my doorway was a miserable little brute with tears of anger in its eyes. I found that the sheer persistence of his voice, that thin whine going on and on, could be more painful than a pneumatic drill going outside the house. In fact, I was making the acquaintance of the Gregory his mother had told me about,—'A parasite, yes, that's the word.'

I had imagined that, once things were better with his father, he would have less time for me. But kids don't operate that way. Grown-ups exist to be played off against each other. Now he had two of us. So now he bragged to me about his daddy, and his satchel, and the wonderful holiday his daddy was going to give him. And to keep his daddy up to scratch, he bragged to him about Harryboy.

It got so that one day I lost my temper and smacked him. I'd looked down on his mother for doing it, but I could no more help myself than she could.

Of course, looking back, my heart is all with the kid. Poor sprat, he lives in a lousy grown-up world. We do a thousand things that hurt and puzzle him. As far as love goes, we are as selfish in sucking it out of him as he is in sucking it out of us. So he fights for himself without scruple.

But this is looking back. When I smacked him, I just felt sick and tired of him. He told me I was horrid, and said he wouldn't play with me any more. I said that was OK with me. A few days later the Deaners went on holiday.

And believe me, I felt a tremendous sense of peace. The mother, the father, the child, I was fed up with all three of them.

There was only one thing wrong with these two peaceful weeks in town. My luck had turned sour. I couldn't do a thing right. I came away from the track night after night with that aching, empty feeling. This is the only time that anything you could call a gambling fever grips me. All day long, between meetings, there gnaws in me the need to bet again, to bet more, for a gambler's logic is that bad luck can't last for ever, and if you don't want to lose the lot you must keep investing till the break comes. Only keep on. More. More. Maybe the next race. You can't tear yourself away. Give up now and you may be throwing away a fortune. So you lose more, and more.

Gus has an office in the West End and I dropped in there one morning, fishing around for information. Gus himself, after a few civilities, I left alone. He was too busy to chat. He is a hard-working business man, respectable, religious, cautious. No gambler he. A bookmaker doesn't gamble. The odds he lays are always inside what he is taking, and he hedges the big ones, maybe at better odds than he is laying. Gus fascinates me. This stout little man, always in a formal dark-brown suit, the home bird, the dullard in conversation, has a mind like a million-pound computer and a public reference library rolled into one. All day long, and all the evening on his stand at the track (his 'joint' he calls it) his brain has to work like an automatic switchboard with ten thousand telephone lines all busy. He is receiving information, talking to people, carrying on an incessant flow of lightning calculations and watching with eyes all round his head, so that he can lay the right odds at the right moment, changing them second by second amid the shouting babble of his competitors. I am stunned with admiration for him. I tried to tell him once, but he honestly doesn't realise that there's anything to it, and he just grunted, 'Ah, you get used to it.'

There was nothing much to be learned from his staff, and when they started to get busy I went out. I walked down Regent Street in the sunshine. Ahead of me I saw someone who seemed familiar, a tall woman in a smart jersey suit of deep lavender, walking with a fine, athletic stride. I caught up with her. It was Marcia.

I moved in on her. She gave me a sharp, sideways look. Then, as if reassured, she smiled, and said 'Hallo.' We went on, without slowing our pace. She said, 'I thought it was someone else. I'm being followed.'

I don't care to be involved in other people's troubles, but I saw no need to run away, and when she offered me a drink I agreed, and we turned in to the Café Royal bar. We sat down. I said, 'Who is it? Hoodlums? The law? I didn't know you were mixed up with either of them.'

'I'm not,' she said, and with a movement of her eyes she directed my attention to the doorway.

The man coming to our table looked about my age, but a real gentleman, black suit, umbrella, thin well-bred face, greying hair. Marcia said, 'My husband.'

He stopped at our table. He said, 'Marcia.'

She said, coldly, 'Hallo, Charles.'

He flickered a glance of appeal at me, but I sat tight. He said, 'Marcia, I thought it might be nice if we had a talk.'

'I'm engaged.'

'How are you keeping?'

'Does it matter?'

'Yes. Yes, Marcia. It does.'

She turned to look across at the bar. 'Where are those drinks?' Then to her husband, 'You're only wasting your time.'

He said to me, 'I wonder if you would excuse us for a few moments.'

Under the table her hand gripped mine like iron. She said to him, 'I won't have you following me any more. I'm telling you for the last time.'

All the time he spoke quietly, and his face was calm. He was the kind who had been brought up to keep it civilised. 'It's quite a while since we met.'

'Charles, I'm warning you. I know people. If you don't leave me alone I'll have every bone in your body broken.'

He stood for a moment in a perplexed silence. Then, 'Marcia, wouldn't you consider coming home?'

'You're mad.'

'I've kept everything as it was for you.'

She laughed. 'Would you like to take me to the country club? You know I slept with every man there. They'd give me a fine welcome.'

Another pause. 'We could—move. I could get a house somewhere else. The bank would transfer me.'

'Charles, go away before I have you thrown out.'

His face was polite. All the pain was in his eyes. He said to me, 'Forgive me, sir, but this lady is my wife. Won't you please—?'

'Charles,' she said. She was leaning forward with her hands clasped on the table, and although her voice was soft it was hard with the same pleasure of cruelty that showed in her eyes. 'I should say that I've been —ed by two thousand men in the last five years. And I love it. There'll be a couple more tonight, and another two thousand before I've finished. Would you like to be my maid? I'd like you to see what I do with them. You and I never got up to such tricks.' Smiling, speaking softly, she began to tell him things, all the dirty things, with all the detail, her eyes watching all the dirty words strike home. He just stood there. He stood there, and I slouched in my chair watching him. She said, 'Now, Harry here, Harry has had me quite a few times.' She told him things about her and me. He just stood there. Then she told me about him, what he had been like. 'Every time he comes,' she said, 'I rub his nose in it. Don't I, Charles? I do all I can to provoke you. I live in hopes of a crime passionel. If only one day you would produce a pistol. But you won't. You'll just go on living in hopes that one day I will let you kiss my feet again.'

He raised his hat to me. So help me, he raised his hat. He said, 'Good day, sir. Keep well, Marcia.' He went out.

She drank her brandy-and-soda off like medicine and signalled for another. She said, 'It's funny. I used to feel sick with hatred just to hear that man breathe. After five years, I still do. Every time he comes.'

'What did he do to you?'

'Nothing. He worshipped me. He still does. I have to make him suffer.'

'You like to?'

'I don't like to. I just do.' She opened her bag for cigarettes. 'The best thing he can do is keep away from me. But he won't.'

She sat puffing out cigarette smoke and staring into it, as if she was alone. She seemed brooding, depressed. She said abruptly, 'Come away with me. I want to go to Goodwood. Will you come?'

'You don't give me much notice.'

'Come on. I don't want to go alone. I'm fed up with town. You'll bring me luck.'

'You want luck, take someone else. I been backing losers for two weeks.'

'Then I'll bring you luck. Come on. I need a change.' She waited. 'Are you broke?'

'Putting it mildly, yes.'

'I'll pay. Don't worry. I'll make you work it out.'

We drove down to the best hotel in Brighton and we went to all four days' racing at Goodwood. When we weren't at the track we went for walks, ate big meals and spent a lot of time in bed. Marcia may have needed a change, but not from that form of exercise.

Brighton was crowded for the Sussex Fortnight, the hotel was full of owners and big punters, and the restaurant was loud with their champagne parties every night. Marcia and I had brought good clothes and I walked among the big shots like one of them. We strolled around the Casino at nights, and with this tall, smart woman at my side, I felt like a duke.

I didn't even have to take money from Marcia. For those few days at the track my luck came back. It was Marcia's luck. She backed by caprice and for a change I followed her, and we won, won, won. In the Casino she wouldn't let me sit down at a table. She was ice-cold, that woman. But at the track she never missed. We won enough to pay our way. I had a full wallet, I spent all my winnings on her, and I felt like a big man.

She was a very relaxed person on holiday. Outside of her wildcat sessions in the bedroom, there was nothing of the whore to be seen in her. She dressed smartly. She talked well. She could pace me in a fast four-mile walk along the promenade. Like me—and this I respect in a woman—she was not afraid to over-eat. She was crazy about antique shops. The crowds swarmed, the sea glittered, and I was on holiday with a lady. Make no mistake—no sentiment was shown between us. But we were good company to each other. We had got far outside our normal lives, and we were in that dream-like state called holiday.

On the last night we took a bottle of brandy up to our room. Three hours later we were still awake and we had drunk a lot of brandy.

Marcia, full of drink, sleep and fulfilment, lay on the bed with an arm hooked round my neck, trying to admire her own fine, long legs. She was barely able to lift them up or to keep her eyes open. She muttered, 'I'm glad it was you.'

'I'm glad, too.'

'It takes a lot to make me fancy a man, Harry.'

'Does it?'

'Yes. You know how I use them? Like sanitary towels. But I fancy you.'

I said, 'Go on, if you'd met someone else that day, someone else would be in this bed.'

'Maybe. But I'm glad it was you.'

She closed her eyes and I thought she was going to sleep, but after a minute she spoke again, in a sleepy, girlish voice. 'I needed this.'

'Don't tell me you overwork.'

'You can laugh. I get so sick and tired.'

'Sick of what?'

'Everything. Of my work, as you call it.'

'I thought you enjoyed it.'

'If you only knew.'

'Go on, you enjoy it.'

She rolled over to face me. 'It? You mean sex? I'm not talking about that. It's the men. They're such a rotten, pitiful lot.' She relaxed, and tightened her arm round my neck. 'Not you.'

'You needn't be tactful.'

'No, really, a few are all right. Americans mostly. At least they're company. Oh, if you only knew, all those fine, upstanding colonels on leave who want to be spanked, and buccaneering business men who can just grunt for a few seconds, and those ever-so-polite country lawyers. I get sick and tired just putting up with them.'

'You don't have to.'

'Don't I? What do I live on?'

'What about your houses?'

She sat up and offered me brandy. I shook my head. She poured some for herself and drank it. 'Harry, I want to be independent. I'll do anything with anybody for a price. For one reason. To make myself independent.'

'But aren't you? You can live on your rents.'

'I mean independent for life. Listen, those slum houses are no use. I get a few years' rent from each and then they're pulled down. Any day a law could be passed to put me out of business. Look how quickly they got the girls off the streets. It could happen. Then where would my living be?' She sipped brandy. 'I need five years, Harry. For another five years I've got to raise every penny I can get. On the game, from houses, any way. Then I shall be free. I've bought a block of flats. It's in a good district, Harry, and it cost big money. It's got a porter, lifts, carpets, oak panelling, wealthy tenants, the lot. It's just not in the same world as my East End houses. It's all legal. I've got a lawyer and an estate agent running the whole thing for me. It's cost me big money, Harry. I won't tell you how many thousands. I got it with a bank loan, and every time I think of that loan I'm frightened. But in five years' time I shall be clear. I shall have an income. I shall be completely free. For life.'

'And then?'

'What do you mean, and then?'

'And then what?'

'And then I'll enjoy life.'

'How?'

'I shall have a nice flat. In Kensington. I shall be one of those enigmatic widows. I shall collect antiques and have other nice women for tea.'

'What about men?'

'I'll cross that bridge when I come to it.'

'I'll tell you something, Marcia. You need your work.'

'No, I don't.'

'Yes, you need to have all those rotten, pitiful men.'

'You're crazy. If you only knew! In five years I shall be free. I'm counting the days.'

'A three a.m. fairy-tale. You need those strangers ringing your doorbell. Each one a question mark. What will he be like? What will he do? You need them like you need air.'

'You're crazy.' But her fatigued eyes were looking at me as if I had made them see something. I touched her breast. Her heart was thumping. 'You're crazy.'

At my touch, she rolled over against me, and pressed her face into my shoulder. She murmured, 'Hold me, Harry.' Her strong arms tightened around me, desperately. 'Hold me. Hold me tighter. Hold me.'

*　　　　*　　　　*

When I woke up the next morning she was still sleeping. In sleep her face looked youthful, a rare thing at her age. I was still heavy in my head from last night, and I remembered what she had said and how she had clutched me, and I looked at her indulgently. I quietly phoned down to Room Service, with a request that had come into my head.

We were having breakfast downstairs that morning, before the journey home. All the waiter brought was early coffee, and when he came in she was sitting up, neat and tidy. He set the tray down, from it he took a glass of water, in which was a bunch of anemones, and put it on her bedside table.

She said, 'What's this?'

The waiter said, 'The gentleman ordered the flowers for you, madam.'

She waited till he had gone, then she took the posy from the glass and threw it across the room. It fell on the floor next to the waste-paper basket. She said, 'The gift is not appreciated.'

'Don't take it to heart.'

'I don't like to be misunderstood. I don't want that sort of thing. From anyone.'

'My mistake, honey. I thought you were human.'

She was pouring coffee and handing me my cup during all this. She looked at the nearly empty brandy bottle and said, 'No wonder I talked too much.'

'Did you talk too much?'

'I told somebody my business. That's a mistake I shan't make again.'

'Your secrets are safe with me.'

'I don't care about you. I'm angry with myself. Perhaps I gave you the impression that I had a vacancy for a ponce?'

'It's not my trade. I'm a Hoffmann presser.'

'I haven't got any vacancies, whatever your trade is.'

She got out of bed. She looked magnificent. Watching her, with the conceit of the last four days in me, I still felt indulgent. She went into the bathroom and came back with her skin pink and glowing. In the mornings she always washed in cold water. I had just crawled out of bed. She picked up her bra and panties. She said, 'Next time you come and see me, Harry, be sure to have your ticket money ready.'

'Sure. I feel better when I pay.'

'How are you fixed now? You've spent all your winnings, haven't you?'

'Don't worry. I had good value for my money.'

She looked at me. Her roll-on was on the floor. She said, 'Give me that.' I handed it to her.

She put it on, sat on the bed and smoothed her nylons up her legs. She said, 'Do these up.'

There was nothing of the coy bedroom invitation in her voice. Thousands of men had seen her body naked, but it was intolerable to her that one man had seen her feelings naked. I knelt down. All the time I was fastening the suspenders to her stockings I looked up into her face and she looked at me.

She stood up, and hunched a silk dress over her shoulders a sixty-guinea Dior number. She said, 'Zip me up.'

I came up behind her, took the zip, and instead of pulling it up I jerked it downwards with all my strength, ripping the back of the dress apart. She stood stock still. Then she moved her shoulders, and when the torn dress fell from her she kicked it into the corner by the waste-paper basket. She went to her suitcase, took out a skirt and a blouse, and put on the skirt. All this time she did not look round at me or say a word. I went into the bathroom.

When I came out she was sitting at the dressing-table, busy at the mirror. Without turning round, she said, 'Harry, what are you going to do?'

'Make a crust.'

'How?'

'How I always do.'

'Would you be interested in a job?'

'Have you changed your mind about a ponce? Or is it that maid's job you spoke to your husband about?'

'Collecting my rents.'

'That's a handsome offer.'

'When you work as a presser, what do you get?'

'Fourteen, fifteen, sixteen a week.'

'You'd get ten. For one morning. It's quite easy. In each house one tenant collects all the rents. He gets a rebate for it. All you have is a dozen calls.'

'Who does it now?'

'I do.'

'You go down there on your own?'

'Why not?'

'Why don't you give it to an agent?'

'It's a hundred and fifty pounds a week. No record for the tax people. I don't trust agents.'

'You trust me?'

'I would trust you, Harry, with money.'

'Thank you. You'll forgive me if I turn the offer down.'

She opened her handbag, took out four five-pound notes and put them on the dressing-table. 'In that case you'll need some stake money.'

I came up behind her. 'Don't be disappointed in me, sweetheart. I'll take it.'

*   *   *

The Deaners had got home before me. Vic and Gregory had caught the sun. Evelyn was the sallow type that never does. Vic gave me a loud, 'Hallo, hallo.' Gregory glanced up at me and got busy again with his toys. There was nothing hostile in his look. He had just forgotten me. Never expect a welcome from a kid after two weeks. By then you are a stranger.

I asked if they'd had a good time. Vic said, 'Lovely!'

Evelyn answered, in a tight voice, 'All right.' I caught Vic flashing her an anxious look. She said, 'Gregory, give Uncle Harry his present.'

Gregory fumbled unwillingly in the sideboard and produced a stick of pink rock. Evelyn said, 'Go on, give it to him.'

Gregory said, 'He doesn't like rock.'

'Don't be greedy,' his mother said. 'There's plenty more for you.'

He held it out, his lips screwed together. I said, 'Thanks, Gregory. Did you like your holiday?'

He didn't answer. Evelyn said, 'Answer Uncle Harry.'

I said, 'It's all right.' Then to Vic, 'Did you have good digs?'

'They weren't bad at all. Plenty of food. Wasn't there?' This was to Evelyn, and I caught the note of appeal. She went on clearing the table. Vic was looking at her. I noticed Gregory. He was looking up at them, from one to the other. I swear that Gregory broke the silence deliberately. 'I've got a net.' He took it out of the corner. 'I catched seaweed in it.'

I said, 'It's a shrimp net, boy.'

'I never catched no shrimps, I catched seaweed.'

'Your dad can take you down to the River Lea,' I said. 'Catch tiddlers in a jar. Did you ever do that, Vic?'

Vic broke the silence which had congealed around him and his wife. 'Oh, often.' He tried again with her. 'Evelyn, are you going to make Harry a cup of tea?'

She walked out into the kitchen with her tray of crockery, and said, as if Vic had not spoken, 'Shall I make you a cup of tea, Harry?'

I said, 'I'll have one later. I got things to do now. Thanks for the rock, kid. I'll keep some for you.' I went upstairs.

Five minutes later Vic knocked at my door. I said, 'How did it go?'

'She won't talk to me.'

I didn't want to know their troubles. I said, 'How did it go with the kid?'

'Wonderful. At least, it could have been. It was lovely with him, honestly. We did everything. I made the most enormous sandcastles for him. We went paddling and rowing, and looking for crabs. I've never enjoyed myself so much as I did on that beach. Not since I was a child myself. Honestly we were great pals. He was ever so proud of me. We could have had such a marvellous time.'

He waited for me to echo, 'Could have?' But I didn't, and he went on. 'Do you know what she told them? The people at the boarding-house. She said we lived at Ilford. She gave her parents' address. She was ashamed to tell them where we really lived.'

'For Christ's sake,' I said, 'who do you get in an eight-pound-a-week boarding-house? The aristocracy?'

'Well, you know, they were sort of office workers, retired people. All that sort. We used to sit in the evenings and talk. We didn't go out, 'cause Gregory was in bed. She used to boast to them. I tried to stop her. She told me to mind my own business, I'd given her nothing to be proud of. She used to describe all her parents' home and so on as if it was our own. And then, just before the end one evening, I let the truth slip out, I couldn't help it, I just mentioned where we lived.'

He was sitting in my armchair by the window, weaving his fingers together and avoiding my eyes, his voice high and desperate. I wondered what point he was trying to come to. He said, 'We had a terrible row in our bedroom that night. We woke Gregory up. She just got demented. She said I'd deliberately humiliated her. She said my whole aim in life was to humiliate her and drag her down. I couldn't shut her up. And then, from the next morning on, she wouldn't talk to me. I tried to talk to her, you know, keep it normal, for Gregory's sake, but every time she just shut her mouth and looked straight in front of her. It spoiled the whole holiday. She's still keeping it up.'

'So I saw.'

'The last two days were awful. All that lovely enjoyment was spoiled. She made us avoid the other guests. She wouldn't say a word to me, at least, she just snapped a word or two now and then when she had to. I begged her to think of the child. She said she was thinking of him, she was thinking of his future. She said she'd talk to me, when I showed I could do something for him. Well, I played with him on the beach. I made out as if nothing had happened. But he knew. I could see he knew. Everything had gone nasty. And it was so nice before.'

Now he was looking straight at me. His eyes were like a begging dog's, and there were tears in them. 'Harry—listen, I don't like to ask you. But you did once offer—Harry, I've never borrowed before. But I've got to do something. I have to do something quickly. She's driving me mad. I just can't stand it any more.'

Of all times, this had to come when I was broke.

He said, 'I'm sure we could move quickly if I could get some key-money. I could even find a house with a small deposit.'

'How much do you want?'

'I don't like to ask, I mean, I would never dream of asking, but I know the money means nothing to you. And you did offer. I'm sure we could get a place if I had—would two hundred be too much?—It's just a loan—I've already tried Evelyn's parents. They've always been ready enough to criticise. As soon as I ask them for help, all they can do is give me reasons why they can't. They have to count every penny. What about me?' He was almost crying now. 'Harry, I feel so humiliated asking you. I've never borrowed before. I would pay you back. Only a little each week, but you could be sure of it back. You see, I'm desperate. I really am. I can't stand this business with Evelyn any more. I've got to have some money.'

I sat and tried to look thoughtful. Now, now of all times!

He said, 'A hundred would do. I'm sure I could manage with a hundred. I shouldn't really take on too much, anyway. Would a hundred be all right?'

I said, 'I've got some heavy commitments just now, Vic, family commitments. My brother-in-law needed help in a hurry. Look, don't worry, boy, don't worry. But you'll have to be patient. I'll see what I can do.'

He said, muffled, 'Yes. Thank you. I do understand. Of course I do,' and let me steer him to the door.

CHAPTER FIFTEEN

It must have been Marcia who brought me the good luck, because as soon as I was on my own in London, my luck went bad again. I couldn't get a break. I was never wiped out. But I never made enough to come away from the track feeling safe for a week or two—just sufficient to pay my daily bills and give me a small stake for the next night. And small stakes forced on me a policy of careful betting, picking favourites for small gains. When I am at the track a raging hunger wakes up in me, to dare all, to make the big killing. But I have to stifle this when I am playing for my rent and dinner money.

I could do nothing for Vic. Luckily he didn't repeat his request. To avoid embarrassment, I tried to see him less often, and I think he sometimes avoided me, out of shame. But when we did meet, he asked questions with his eyes, and occasionally I was forced to assure him that I had the matter in hand, I only had to clear up my family commitments first.

I thought things would be better for him when the de Souzas suddenly sprang it on us that they were moving. Together with a cousin of Milly's, they had taken a small house over in Stoke Newington, sharing the deposit. In a few weeks they were gone, and a single man moved in, a Pole with a face like a prison door. He was one of those frightening solitaires who go in and out of a house at strange hours, always silent; to this day I know nothing about him. His room door was always locked. He never used the gas stove on the landing.

It choked Evelyn that the de Souzas could get a house before her. This black man, this workman, who came home in overalls and grime, had got a house! They were all as bad as each other, the workpeople who lived down this street, with their cars, and their holidays abroad, and their washing-machines, and buying drinks all round on Saturday night at the pub on the corner. They poured out money like water, those unions were always getting more for them, and Evelyn, the daughter of a decent middle-class family, had to go without, to trudge up and down the market saving pennies, to live in a mean flat below her proper level. She became even more insistent that they must move. Her boycott of Vic had crumbled, but her eyes always accused him, she sat over her sewing like a baleful cat, wearing him down with silence. From time to time her hysteria burst out in fresh demands. From my room I heard their voices raised, doors slamming.

Gregory lived his own life. He had never been so quiet. He sat for hours in the middle of his toy town. He sat for hours in front of the television set. Sometimes he sat in the front room bay window watching the street happenings. He said nothing, but I believe that he took in everything through those large watchful eyes. It sometimes happened when I was downstairs with them that suddenly, breaking the normal drone of conversation, Evelyn would spit a sneer at her husband, he would spit a remark back at her—and then the ordinary conversation would drone on. But in those few seconds I would notice the instant alertness with which the child looked up, first at one, then at the other of his parents, his dark eyes inscrutable, like a pitiless little judge.

He came upstairs to me quite often, friendly again but withdrawn, with no displays of affection. I didn't want him round my neck. I didn't want his parents' troubles, or his. Nor did I want to be an influence on him. At his age, everything we do leaves a dent on the child. I didn't want to share the responsibility.

Now I come to an incident that occurred one Sunday morning. The sun was shining. I had gone for a walk. This incident began (Vic told me all about it later) with a promise.

At seven o'clock Gregory was in his parents' bed. They were both in a good mood. He was well-behaved. He sat between their pillows, put an arm round each of them, something he had not often done since he was small, and asked them to take him on a picnic. They drowsily tried to put him off with 'perhaps' and 'we'll see', but he wheedled in his most seductive voice. Vic said he would take him out later, but Gregory said, 'I want you and Mummy to take me out.' At last they agreed. He cried, 'You promise?' I could imagine the brightness of triumph shining in the kid's face, for to this day I am convinced that the whole idea was a piece of diplomacy on Gregory's part. Now he must have seen himself as the designer of a great and wonderful coup which would put an end to all fears, insecurities and unhappinesses.

He insisted, 'You promise, Mummy? You do promise?'

His mother said, 'Yes, I promise. Now do be quiet and let Mummy have a little rest.'

They got up, washed, and went into the other room for breakfast. All this time Gregory carried on an earnest and intellectual conversation with his father. The main subject of discussion was God.

Gregory was intensely interested in three fundamental subjects—death, birth and God.

On this particular morning he was arguing with his father. Vic and Evelyn had opposite views on many subjects, and for the most part they were tolerant of each other, even proud of their ability to differ. Evelyn was an all-round conservative. Vic called himself progressive.

'But supposing,' Vic insisted—they were just finishing breakfast—'supposing there isn't a God?'

'But there is, Daddy.'

'Have you ever seen him?'

Gregory pondered. Then, 'If I had never seen Harryboy, Daddy, there would still be a Harryboy.'

Evelyn, with a glower of triumph that was deeper than mere pride in her child—her bitterness was something constant, underlying even her good moods like the heat and glare of volcanic fires—said, 'Clever darling,' and kissed the child.

Gregory counter-attacked. 'Daddy, who made the world, then?'

'Nobody made the world.'

'How can nobody make anything?'

'Well, you see, Greg, this is what happened. Once a little bit of gas came off the sun. It got flung out into space and it whirled round and round, and that made it get shaped like a ball, and it cooled down, and it became the world. And then the rain filled up all the holes on it and that was the sea. And then little fish swam about in the sea, and some of them crawled up on the land, and they kept on getting bigger and changing till they were men and women—'

All through this Gregory was staring at his father, until at last, in a cunning, confidential voice, he interrupted, 'You don't really believe that silly old story, do you, Daddy?'

Evelyn laughed out loud in derision and triumph. She said, 'It serves you right, stuffing the child's head with nonsense.'

Vic said, 'I'm not stuffing his head with nonsense. I don't mind what he believes, but I like to hear him working it out for himself.'

'A fine example you are, you and your crazy ideas.'

'I don't think you're in a position to criticise me. Do you ever open a book? I take an intelligent paper in on Sundays. Do you ever look at it?'

'Do I ever have time to? Do I have any chance to keep up intelligent interests in this dirt-trap? I used to have time to read. I used to have the money to belong to a good library. That was when I lived a civilised life.'

'Before I dragged you down?'

'You said it, not me.'

Vic forced himself not to answer. He took his books from the bureau and started to set them out on the table. Evelyn went into the kitchen. Gregory followed her. She was running hot water into the sink, spilling detergent into the water, and heaping dirty linen on a chair nearby. He looked back into the other room. His father was peering into a book and writing.

'Mummy, when are we going on our picnic?'

'I've got work to do, dear. Go and play.'

'Daddy—?'

'Ask your mother. She's the one who's changed her mind.'

'Mummy, are we going on a picnic?'

'No, Gregory. I don't feel like it. Go and play.'

'But, Mummy—'

'Gregory, please, your mummy's very upset. Now leave me alone, please.'

Vic said, 'We did promise—'

'Well, then, he's got to learn to be disappointed, like grown-ups. I've had promises made to me, too, in my time.'

So Evelyn went on with her washing and Vic went on with his work, and neither of them paid attention when Gregory opened the cupboard where his toybox was. They didn't pay any attention a minute later when he went out of the room.

A little while later, a heavy scraping sound from the hall attracted Vic's attention. He went out. Gregory was standing on a chair opening the street door. Although it was a warm day he wore his duffle-coat. Over his shoulder was slung his beloved satchel. In the satchel (which the kid, whose fingers were not yet dexterous, had left open) were a slice of toast taken from the breakfast table, a comic book and Gregory's favourite miniature car.

Vic said, 'Hey, what's this?'

Gregory said, 'I'm going away.'

Vic called, 'Evelyn! Evelyn!' To the kid he said, 'Where are you going?'

'To Australia.'

Evelyn came out into the hall. Vic said, 'He's going away to Australia.'

Evelyn said, 'Why are you going away, dear?'

The kid did not answer, and she said to Vic, 'Poor little darling. Doesn't he look pathetic.'

Vic picked him up off the chair. 'Did Mummy and Daddy disappoint you, son? Never mind.' He kissed him, and said to Evelyn, 'He looks such a little scrappet sometimes. He's only a baby.'

Gregory screamed, 'I'm not a baby,' the tears burst out of him like a sprinkler switched full on, and he writhed down out of his father's arms. He ran into the bedroom and slammed the door behind him.

Vic snapped the latch of the street door in case Gregory tried to get out again. He and Evelyn, their moods melted again, smiled at each other sentimentally and went back into the kitchen. Vic said, 'Let him have his cry. We must take him on that picnic now.'

Evelyn said, 'Yes, I'll get ready. Wait a minute, I know what he likes.' She took a fairy cake from a tray in the pantry, opened a pot of strawberry jam, split the cake and filled it with jam. She said, 'I'll take it to him.'

She went into the hall and tapped on the bedroom door. 'Gregory, may I come in?' Silence from inside the room. 'Gregory, we are going on the picnic. I've got something for you.' Silence. She opened the door. The kid was not there. She called to her husband. 'He must have crept upstairs to Harry.' She went to the foot of the stairs and called, 'Gregory! Gregory!'

There was no response. Vic said, 'Leave him up there. He'll come down.'

Vic went back to his books. Evelyn went into the kitchen to make picnic sandwiches.

Soon after, I came home. I couldn't get in because the door was latched. I rang the bell, and Vic opened. He said, 'I didn't know you were out. Gregory went upstairs. I thought he was with you.'

I said he was probably sitting up in my room, and I went up. He was not there. I came out on to the landing and tried the door of the Pole's room. It was locked. For a moment I had vague fears, but the room was dead silent. I called to Vic that Gregory was not up here. Vic came up. He said, 'It's funny. He couldn't have got out of the street door without me hearing, or the bedroom window—' I had told Vic about this—'It's locked.'

I was puzzled. Vic was staring at the fanlight on to the roof. It was open, as it now was on every dry day, and the ladder leaned up against it just as Joe de Souza had left it. He said, 'He couldn't have,' and then, 'I'll just have a look.'

He went up the ladder, through the fanlight opening and said, 'He's not on the roof. Silly to think he could have got up here.' Then, 'Oh, my God!'

He scrambled out on to the roof. I went up after him. Evelyn was coming upstairs.

I got out on to the roof and stood beside him. He was staring up, aghast, his mouth open.

The houses in Ingram's Terrace are all sorts, built to the needs of their first buyers. Next to ours is a house two stories higher. A wall runs up sheer from our roof to theirs, and to this wall is clamped an iron fire ladder to give an escape from the next-door attic.

Against the sky, on the roof above us, stood Gregory. Where he stood there was no parapet. If he should walk to the front of the roof, overlooking the street, he would come up against a parapet only as high as his knees—low enough for him to fall over.

Deathly white, Vic forced himself to wave, and he muttered to me, 'Don't shout.'

He walked slowly towards the foot of the ladder, and he spoke as gently as he could to his son. 'Don't go away, darling. Wait for Daddy. I want to come up. Will you wait and help me get up?'

Gregory, calm and interested, looked down. Evelyn was on the roof now. Her hands were clasped tight across her breast and she was trembling.

Vic started up the ladder. Gregory walked away towards the front parapet. Vic called, 'Don't move, darling. Please, Gregory, don't move.'

Gregory called back, 'It's ever such a long way down to the street. You come and have a look.'

Evelyn called, 'Come down, Vic. Let me go.' To me she said, 'He shouldn't be up there.'

Vic had stopped. He was clinging to the ladder. I waited. He didn't move. His arms above him were rigid, his hands locked to the steel rung. Evelyn said, 'He can't stand heights. Oh, my God, what shall we do?'

I called, also keeping my voice gentle, 'Gregory!'

He said, 'What's the matter with my daddy?'

'Never mind. Come and watch me climb up.'

Gregory hesitated, then he came away from the parapet and walked back to the top of the ladder.

As I climbed past Vic he muttered, 'I'm sorry. I'm sorry. I can't stand heights.' I said softly, 'You're all right. Just let yourself down.' I called up to Gregory, 'If you wait there I'll come up and give you a pickyback.' Vic was muttering, 'I get dizzy. I can't help it, I get dizzy.'

I called, 'Watch me. I'm coming up now to give you a pickyback. Do you want a pickyback down the ladder?'

I hoisted myself on to the higher roof. Gregory put his arms round my neck and planted a long hard kiss on the side of my head. He said, 'My daddy's frightened. You're not frightened, are you, Harryboy?'

'Why did you come up here?'

'To talk to God.'

'God can hear you just as well if you kneel down on your bed.'

'No he can't. He's in the sky. I did try, and he didn't hear me.'

'What did you tell him?'

'About my mummy and daddy.'

I stood on the ladder, with my shoulders just above the roof level. 'Do you want that pickyback? Come on. Get on.' With one hand I helped him on. He hung on my back, a dead weight, and his arms were round my neck. I started down the ladder.

So there I was, with Gregory riding on my back again.

CHAPTER SIXTEEN

There was no break in my luck. The principle in gambling is that if you have enough capital to see you through, you must come up right in the end. It stands to reason you can't lose for ever. But you have to keep on. You have to have the cash to keep on. And sometimes you have to keep losing for an awful long time.

Vic hung around. From time to time he nervously dropped a hint. But by now, irritated by my own troubles, I was getting sick of his. What was he putting this burden on me for? To save his life? All he had to grumble about was a nagging wife. So? If you want the woman, you got to put up with the nagging. I should buy him out of his trouble? They didn't like their flat. Terrible, I cried for them, two nice rooms and a kitchen in a respectable house, and the wife turned her nose up at it. For this I was supposed to break my head?

Why should I make excuses? Why should I be ashamed he might find I had no money? I would give him the stern line, I decided. I would tell him I had enough troubles in my own family, I could not take on his. What harm would it do him to live here for another year?

We avoided the issue till a Sunday morning at the beginning of September. Vic caught me in the hall and said, in a strained attempt at joviality, that we hadn't had one of our walks for quite a while. So we went out to the park with Gregory.

In the street we talked about nothing special. When we got on to the Downs, Vic led us into the big field. At the other end, a good five hundred yards away, some big boys were flying kites. Vic pointed them out to Gregory, and said, 'Go on, let's see how fast you can get there,' and Gregory raced away from us.

Neither of us said anything till the kid was some distance off. Then Vic said, 'Harry, have you been able to, er—?'

I didn't help him.

'That business we were talking about. Have you been able to do anything?'

I said, 'Frankly, no,' and shut up. Vic walked at my side, his head hunched glumly down.

'I don't know what to say,' he said. 'I don't like even to raise it with you. But you did give me to understand—'

'I'm very sorry, Vic. I'm far too involved in my own commitments. And frankly, I must say, I don't think your troubles are that bad. What you need to do is to take your wife in hand. Give her a good talking-to.'

'Maybe you think I've got no right to complain,' he said, 'but you did promise me. Don't you realise—? I thought I had you to count on.'

'I didn't promise you, Vic. Evelyn's just got to be sensible and realise it'll do you no harm to stay where you are.'

'But it's got nothing to do with that. I counted on you.'

'I'm sorry. You'll have to work out your plans without counting on me.'

He said, 'It's too late,' and walked on in a glum silence.

'What do you mean?'

He didn't answer.

'What do you mean, it's too late?'

'I meant what I said, it's too late.'

His face was a confession of trouble, his mouth turned down like a child's with self-pity. He was looking around him, everywhere but at me. He wanted me to coax it out of him. I didn't try and after a few more seconds he said, dully, 'I've taken the money. From work.'

We walked on a few paces. I said, 'That was a silly thing to do. Still, if you've put down a deposit you can always get it back.'

'I didn't put down a deposit,' he walked another few paces. 'I've lost it. On the dogs.'

Gregory, a little coloured bundle, was bobbing ahead of us, close to the boys with the kites. As I looked at him I felt that he was in one world, we were in another. I said, 'When did this begin?'

There was a childish bitterness in Vic's voice. 'If you hadn't been so busy avoiding me lately, you'd know I've been out two or three nights a week. It was when I saw you were avoiding me that I got desperate.'

'How much have you lost?'

'Two hundred and twenty pounds,' he burst out. 'I was desperate.'

'Sure.'

'I didn't know what to do.'

'So you did this? Brilliant.'

'I didn't mean to. I only took twenty pounds at first. But then—'

'All right, don't tell me. But then you lost it, and you had to borrow another twenty to try and get it back. And then you lost again, and you had to take some more, and now you don't know how to stop.'

'I have stopped.'

'Mazzeltov. So what are you going to do now?'

'I don't know.'

'You'll have to pay it back.'

'Don't be absurd, how can I?'

'At least you can put back a couple of pounds a week. You'll have to tell Evelyn some story why you're giving her less.'

'But I can't. It's all a nightmare, Harry. I never thought I could do a thing like this. I was desperate. I didn't know what I was doing.'

'You told me already. Look, why don't you come clean with the boss and arrange to pay him back?'

'Do you think he'd give me a start as a company secretary after that? Or even recommend me? My career would be finished. And I've worked so hard.'

I just grunted, and we walked on in silence.

'Harry, I've only got a month.'

'What do you mean, only a month?'

'The auditors come in next month. They do a full stock-taking. We have it every year, it has to be finished before the Christmas rush starts. I could cover up if it wasn't for them. Harry, I've got one month.'

'You should have thought of that before you took the money.'

'It was Evelyn. I was going mad.'

'You'll go mad when your boss finds out.'

'You don't have to talk to me like that. You not lending me the money was the last straw. And you took me, didn't you?'

'Are you blaming me now?'

'It's funny, isn't it? If you hadn't taken me racing, none of this would have happened. Oh God, how do you think I felt when I saw you collecting all that money from the book-makers?'

'I warned you.'

'You warned me. Yes, and you make a fortune yourself.'

I laughed at this. How could I help it? He cried out, in a rage, 'All right, you can laugh. You're stuffed with money, you don't know what it's like to be without it. You're full of talk, but you're not so ready to part with it when it comes to the pinch, are you? My God, how do you think I felt? I was going crazy for money, and you showed me hundreds, hundreds just being picked up, just for guessing a winner.'

'How did you lose it?'

'How did I lose it? I backed the wrong dogs. How did you think? You told me the summary of selections was the best thing to follow. You said if the most tipsters agreed on a dog it must stand the best chance. So I followed it.'

'And you just backed to win?'

'Well, what else?'

I sighed. 'I don't know where to start telling you,' I said. 'Look, I have a friend, he is a walking encyclopaedia about dogs. He can tell you the result of every race for the last five years. I heard him the other night at the track, for a half-dollar bet, name the sire and dam of every dog running that night—forty-eight dogs. That man is a gambler. And he is broke. Broke. What do you people think a track is? An orchard with money growing on the trees? My God, you think you're the only one. I see crowds of you pouring down the hill at Harringay, pushing past the turnstiles, all you silly greedy faces. Millions of you. You buy a newspaper and you think you know. For God's sake, a gambler spends his whole day studying form. All day he talks to other gamblers before he makes up his mind. He has been doing this for anything up to thirty years. He bets every way up you can imagine, forecasts, reverse forecasts, place bets, combinations, he uses one bet to guarantee him against another, he bets on the dogs and the horses, he bets doubles, trebles, accumulators, he can put on If Cash, Any to Come, Up and Down, Round the Clock, Rounders, Roundabouts, Round Robins, he can bet on owners, he can bet on trainers, he can bet on jockeys, he studies pedigree, he invents systems a professor wouldn't understand. And he still loses. For crying out loud, man, am I making you hear me? He still loses.' For a moment I lost my breath. 'So you, you greenhorn, you babe in arms, you poor innocent nit, you think you can just walk in and win?'

It was a few moments before he answered. 'It's a bit late to tell me all that. What do I do now?'

'Don't ask me.'

'I could go to prison for this.'

'Too true. It's a catching disease among punters. I've known two or three get copped for it. Six months is about what you'd get.'

'Well, for God's sake, help me.'

'Vic, I'm not your family. You must ask them.'

'I dare not. I dare not even let Evelyn know.'

'She's your wife.'

'I couldn't. I really couldn't. Besides, my mother's got nothing—'

'Her family aren't so badly off.'

'Ha! Do you know the truth about Evelyn's family? I'll tell you what sort of civil servant her father is. He's what they call a Temp. The lowest grade. He just serves at the rates counter. Actually, it's not even the civil service at all. They haven't got two pennies to rub together. They've got their house. But that's on a twenty-five-year mortgage, and not paid off yet.'

'Vic, you'll have to confide in Evelyn. The kid'll be going to school next term. She can get a job. You can take a loan and pay it back.'

'Where could we get a loan? On what security? All right, you lend me. I'll pay you back. I swear I will. However long it takes. I swear I'll pay you back.'

We had nearly reached the kite-flyers. Gregory came running back to us. He hurled himself like a little rugger player against my legs. 'Harryboy, if I held the string of that big kite, would it take me up in the sky?'

'Not if you kept your feet wide apart on the ground. You're a big boy now.'

'Like this?' He put his feet out wide.

'That's OK.'

'Shall I go and ask him?'

'You go and ask him.'

He ran off. The big boy let him hold the string and he stood there, legs planted grimly apart as if he feared to leave the earth, tugging at the string and making the kite dance in the sky. His face was lifted up to watch, beautiful with a child's wonderment.

Vic's whine broke into my thoughts. 'What could I tell him if I got into trouble? What do they tell a kid when his daddy's in prison? God Almighty, I want to kill myself sometimes. Then I tell myself it would make things even worse for him.'

I was still looking at the child. I said, 'How long did you say you'd got before they rumble you?'

So now I had to find two hundred and twenty pounds. In a month. As always happens my luck, previously bad, become diabolical.

I am a well-known person at the London tracks and I have always enjoyed the privilege of not having to put money down when I bet with a bookie on the course. I had just to give him a signal and the bet was on. Afterwards we settled one way or the other. But now there were a few bookies, at this track or that, I had to avoid. I owed them money. If I didn't pay up soon I would be branded as a knocker, a malt who didn't honour his debts. And believe me, a gambler can well say, 'He that takes from me my good name takes everything.'

I borrowed around from the fellows I knew. But from these, too, I could only take casual fivers, small stake money. And borrowing creates a bad impression.

For that idiot, that little pisher, I was in trouble.

All right, you know why I was doing it. But I could have got away. All I had to do was pack my bags and move to another house. Distance is a great healer for the human conscience.

Instead I stayed. The little boy came upstairs and played with me and we both had a good time. I think I had reached the point where I needed to play tigers with him, and snakes-and-ladders, to forget my troubles.

His visits were now in the evenings, before he went to bed. In the days I was a busy man. Thanks to his genius of a father, I was working again. Five days a week I was in the garment factory, operating a Hoffmann press. On Saturdays I went collecting rents for Marcia.

It was strictly business now with Marcia. When I went to her flat to ask for the job, or when I called there each week with the money, you would never think I had been in that place as a popular paying customer, or that we had been on a holiday together. She didn't ask me any questions the first time I turned up. She just looked me over, nodded, and began to give instructions in the voice she would have used to a stranger. I got that same indifferent look and that same cold voice every time. It suited me like that and I treated her the same way.

I saved all I could. I had my rent to pay, and five cheroots a day—say, twenty-five shillings a week—is basic with me. But I halved my food bill by eating at the Italian café instead of the salt beef restaurant. From my wages I could save six or seven pounds a week, and there was also Marcia's weekly ten pounds.

So? What should I do with it? Save it up and give it to Vic? How much could I give him in four weeks? Seventy quid at the most.

No, there was only one way. For a gambler there is always only one way. With my sixteen-seventeen pounds a week I went to the tracks every night.

Now usually a man goes—a gambler I mean—to the track in a mood of not caring. Win, lose, it's all in a lifetime. And sometimes he wins. But why is it that when he goes *caring*—when he needs the money, when he must have a win, when his lips are dry and his heart running too fast as the dogs streak out of the traps, when he grinds one hand in the other and thinks profane prayers—he never wins?

You reach a point where you have lost so often that it seems impossible you can lose any more. It is sheer, staring, obvious commonsense that you *must* win next time. And having lost, lost, lost, lost, lost, you wait for the next wage packet so that you can hurry to the track—and by now you are hurrying like a stupid, eager, knownothing punter—to place the bets that must, this time they must, they positively must, win. Once upon a time you were calm, complacent when you went to the track. You had a four-course kosher dinner in your belly, you shared a cab with a crowd of the boys, and on the way you joked, laughed, told the ancient tall stories of the track. Now you hasten there alone, and because, precisely because of the incredible, endless run of losses you have suffered, you are breathless now with wild and crazy hopes. Heroin, cocaine, reefers, are baby's sweets compared with gambling. What an irony it was that because of Vic, an innocent goomp who had caught the gambling fever, I—Harryboy Boas, the old hand—was infected with it, too.

Night after night I went with a hot tip, a racing certainty that must save me. (Save Vic, save his little boy.) And every time something went wrong. You have a marvellous dog. He is going to skate home. You know his form, he always breaks away fast, gets a clear lead at the first bend and no one can get near him for the rest of the way. So what happens? He is pushing out of the pack when some scrubber, some no-good dog that doesn't stand a chance, some cripple, takes a fancy to nose him and for a second he falters. Then he picks up, but too late, another dog has got the lead. And yours comes up to him like a bullet, and strains at his tail, to inch alongside, and you are having heart failure. But what's the use? In a sport where races are won in hardly more than thirty seconds, and the finish is so close that the winner often gets in only by a half-length or a photo-finish, your dog has lost when he lost that precious second.

So again and again, when you have worked out the impregnable combination of bets that must give you a winner, the unforeseen, the accident happens, the dog changes feet, or for the first time in fifty-six races he runs wide on the bend, or some outsider by a neurotic quirk cuts in fast to the rails and stays ahead, and once more, incredibly, you have lost. To you it seems like Greek tragedy. The simple truth is, of course, that in dog racing nothing is foreseeable.

The days were slipping by dangerously. A haggard Vic waited for me every time I came downstairs. I went to see Gus at his office.

I asked him for two hundred pounds. He said, 'I'll take two hundred pounds and put a match to it. It'll save time and misery.'

'I want it for a friend.'

'Harry, you got to tell me stories now? For gambling you want it.'

'Gus, I swear it's not for gambling. It's for a friend in trouble.'

'If it was for you, and I thought you were telling the truth, I would give you the money. But for a friend? Why should I worry about your friend? My family is my worry.'

'I've guaranteed this fellow.'

'You shouldn't guarantee. You're so successful yourself? You signed anything?'

For a moment I was going to lie. But with this tubby, honest man, sitting across the desk looking at me mournfully, it stuck in my throat. 'No.'

'So, Harry, I'll save you money. Forget the guarantee.' We sat for a minute. He said, 'When you want money, Harry, it is an unkindness to help you.' Another pause, to listen to his chesty breathing. He said, 'So how are you getting on?'

'I'm working.'

'Thank God. Harry, I only want to see you settle down. Go steady a few months, find a nice homely woman, show me you can work decent like another man, and I'll do everything for you. Everything. Money. A house. A business. Everything you desire. Only so you should stop giving your sister unhappiness.'

W hen I got the rent-collecting job from Marcia I did not want her to think I was broke. She might not have trusted me. So I told her I was working steady right through the winter, playing it careful at the tracks, and putting away all the money I could till the spring. Then I was thinking of going abroad, somewhere warm. I had mentioned the idea to her before and she believed it.

The day after I spoke to Gus I went on my collecting round. The evening between had been as bad as ever at the track. Vic was like a white-faced ghost in the house, with sunken cheeks and fatigued, accusing eyes. It seemed to me as if anyone who saw him ought to be able to read his story in his face. Now I, in turn, was getting so that I couldn't stand the situation any more.

I collected a hundred and sixteen pounds that morning. Surely it will be no surprise to you to learn what I did next. To say I did it for Vic is stretching the truth. In all my years as a professional I had always kept myself under some control. But now to put money in my pocket was like putting a full bottle in the pocket of an alcoholic.

I was supposed to take the money to Marcia before one o'clock. Instead I went into Bloom's. There was nothing in my head, only a pressure. I had a sick feeling and I couldn't eat a meal. I ordered a salt beef sandwich, and I had to cut the fat off and smother it with mustard before I could get it down. I sat looking at the clock and pretending I didn't know what I was waiting for.

At two o'clock I got up and walked down Aldgate like a zombie, with the racing middays folded in my hand. I walked into a betting shop in Great Alie Street. There were meetings at Haydock and Kempton Park that afternoon, and I got there in time to put my money on the first race at Kempton.

My chest was full of that tight, hysterical strain of hope, but underneath it was a deep, deep, sickening pit of darkness, the knowledge of destruction. I stood in that shabby crowd against the counters, in thick cigarette smoke, and the unemotional voice on the loud-speaker taunted me. I went right through the card at Kempton without a winner.

In the evening I went to the dog tracks and did the rest of Marcia's money in. I walked home broke, and as usual I had a feeling that defies any name but that of relief.

I had to say something to Marcia. I rang her number next morning but got no reply. I went back to my room and was reading the paper when there was a knock on the door.

It was Evelyn Deaner. She wore a blue flowered dressing-gown in some thin, shiny material, and a pair of red mules which exposed her feet as large and ugly with crooked yellow toes. She said, 'May I come in?'

'Sure.'

'Are you busy?'

'No. Come in and have a cup of tea.'

'Thanks.' She stood uncertainly, just inside the door. 'I finished my work. Vic's out for the morning. He's gone to his mother with Gregory. I just felt lonely down there.'

'Sit down.'

She hesitated. 'You don't mind?'

I was filling the kettle. 'I always think you work too much. Have a rest. I'll make you a cup of tea.'

She sat down primly on the edge of my bed. 'You keep it nice up here.'

'The old man sweeps out. I just make the bed.'

'Do you like living on your own?'

'I wouldn't like living any other way.'

'You're a funny chap. Do you really think I work too much?'

'I never see you stop.'

'I try to keep a good home. Though I don't see the point of it here. Not till we get a place of our own.'

She sat upright. Her fingers were wrestling each other in her lap. If you have ever seen a shy person suffering agonies in company, speaking too loudly, too jerkily, putting on facial expressions like a bad actor, this was Evelyn. She had never come up to see me before, and I couldn't believe that she had done so because she fancied an hour's company. And it must be something urgent if she let me see her in that get-up. She fell silent. I was embarrassed. I said, 'Gregory's getting a big boy. I expect you'll be glad when he starts school.'

'Oh, I will. Thank heaven they've agreed to take him in January. Sometimes they make you wait till Easter.'

'I think he'll like it.'

'He'll have to learn to do what he's told. He won't like that.'

And we chatted on. We drank tea, and for twenty minutes we chatted on. She sat on the edge of my bed, stiff and upright, chattering inanities too loudly, and every so often she would run out of things to say, and the muscles in her cheeks would work with desperation as she tried to think of something, and then she would come out with some other idiotic remark, and it would go on.

I wanted to get rid of her. But I was sorry for her. I was puzzled. She was obviously trying again and again to bring herself to say something, and losing her nerve each time. I wondered if she knew about Vic.

Another silence. She was looking away from me unhappily. To help her, I said, 'Fancy a drink?'

I had whisky and brandy on my corner table, and some glasses. She was silent for another moment, then she blurted out, 'I would like a drink.'

I gave her a whisky. I gave it to her as she asked, neat. She sat on the edge of my bed, her knees pressed together under the dressing-gown, and nursed the glass in her two hands. Holding the glass seemed to enable her to sit in peace without talking. She sipped, and sat there, thinking.

I said, 'What is it, Evelyn?'

A pause, then: 'It's about Vic. I'm worried about him.'

This did not surprise me. I kept quiet. She said, 'I'm sure he's ill or something.'

So she didn't know. 'Have you talked to him?'

'What about?'

'To find out what's worrying him.'

'No, I haven't.' She ran out of courage, and to give her some more, I poured more whisky into her glass. She sipped some, and said, 'I thought you might know. He does talk to you a lot.

'You're his wife.'

'Yes.' She looked around her, then at me. 'We don't really talk much, though.'

'Wouldn't it be a good idea if you did?'

She drank her whisky in silence. Then, 'It's easier said than done. It's funny, you can talk to someone all day, but it's never about anything.' She laughed. 'We have rows. I don't have to tell you that.'

'You don't have rows all the time.'

'No, the rest of the time, it's "What's on the telly?" or "Close the window" and that sort of thing. Do you think he's ill?'

'He could have something on his mind.'

'You don't know what it is?'

'No, I don't. I think you should try and have a talk with him.'

She held out her empty glass and said, 'Please?' as if she was asking for another nip of courage. She had already emptied it twice. The liquor had brought a pink flush to her cheeks and, absurdly, to the tip of her nose.

When I had filled it she leaned back and made herself comfortable against the pillows. 'I can talk to other people more easily than I can to him. I mean, I can talk to you. I don't feel shy talking to you.' She finished the whisky. 'Oh, I wish we could afford this. It's ever so good for you. It makes you feel so good.' A pause. 'He'll be at his mother's all the morning. He puts the dinner on for her.' She laughed. 'It makes him very happy, waiting on his mother. So you can't tell me anything about him?'

'He's the one to tell you.'

'I don't want to talk to him.' The little-girl petulance she put on, her bright grimace, were a reminder that she was probably quite unused to liquor. 'I want to talk to you.'

'OK. We've got the whole morning. What shall I get for Gregory's birthday? There's not much time.'

'Oh no, I want to talk to you about much more interesting things than Gregory. It's not often I get an hour off. You know, I think I'll have another drink.'

I couldn't refuse. She was not a child. She had one knee up on the bed, with her arms round it, and she was smiling at me with the flirtatious silliness of a woman who is not used to liquor. She said, 'I can always talk after a drink. It warms right through you. It takes all your troubles away. I could do with something like that, believe me. Tell me about you.'

'You're not interested in me.'

With a dreadful gaiety: 'Oh, yes I am. Surprised?'

Now, I may sound so far like the kind, patient friend of the family. But that morning I was full of my own worries, yes, and fears. While this female nit was posturing on my bed I was racking my brains what to do about Marcia. It was all I could do to keep my temper. I said, 'Evelyn, whisky makes you love the whole world. But apart from that, you don't like me at all. You like me like you like a beetle. Now I'll tell you what, take the bottle, take it downstairs, and have a drink with Vic this evening. You'll both feel better. You have a drink or two, and you'll both talk.'

She said, 'Come on, be a sport, tell me all about you. I've heard about some of your goings-on from Vic. You took him to see one of your women once. She was one of your women, wasn't she? He said she was very sophisticated. I can imagine that. You sleep with a lot of women, don't you?'

I stood up. She sat on the bed, hugging her knee, her head on one side with a crazy, pathetic smile. I could see now that she had done her hair and put some red on her lips, but her skin still had that muddy morning look and her dressing-gown hung flat on her. She held out her glass with a coy little noise. I took it and put it on the table. She said, 'Meanie. Why did you take Vic to see that woman? Were you leading him into evil ways?' A high laugh. 'I'd give you a putty medal if you could lead my husband into any evil ways.'

I said, 'You go downstairs and get dressed before your men get home.'

Oh, that high giggle! 'I ought to get dressed. I've only got my nightie on. That's all I've got on under this. I should get dressed, shouldn't I?'

I took her by the arms and lifted her up. 'OK. Blow.'

She let herself hang limp, and she kept on giggling. 'I knew you were strong. Your fingers are like iron. I bet I'll bruise. What shall I tell my husband if I bruise?' Another giggle. 'He won't be home for hours. Really. Aren't you interested?' I was already pushing her to the door, her feet stumbling under her. 'All right, all right. I can take a hint. I'm very flattered, I'm sure. I can see how much I attract you.'

I opened the door, but she turned round to face me and gripped my arms hard. The tears began to run down her face. 'Harry, I'm not asking much. Why not?'

I lost my temper. 'In the first place, I have a good principle—never do it on your own doorstep. In the second place, Vic is a friend of mine and he is also your husband.'

'My husband? That's a good one.' A shaky, unhappy laugh came through her weeping. 'A fat lot of use he is to me in bed.'

'I've heard a different version from him.'

'So he's been talking about me. What has he been saying? Tell me what fine old all-male chats you've been having about me.'

'Never mind that. You give him a break, you might get more from him.'

'I don't want anything from him. I'm fed up with him. I don't care if he never touches me again. It's you I think of all the time. All the time. I do hate you. You're a big, ugly brute, you're horrid. But it makes me hurt inside just to think of you. Harry, I'm not asking much. You shouldn't be on your own like this. You need someone in the house to look after you. I'd do all your housework for you.'

I had forced her out on to the landing, and I was pulling her claws off. She moaned, 'Please. I wouldn't be a bother. No one would know.'

'All right,' I said, 'I'm going out. Now get downstairs to your own place. And don't come up here any more.'

It all faded out of her in a long, trembling sigh. She wiped her nose and eyes, pulled her dressing-gown close across her neck like a woman whose modesty is offended, smiled like a human being and said wryly, 'Now I suppose you'll have another one of your all-male chats with Vic.'

I calmed down, too. 'Forget it, Evelyn. I've forgotten it already. It never happened.'

She turned away and slummocked downstairs without looking back. I went into my room.

*   *   *

I was getting ready to go out that evening when I heard the bang of the street-doorknocker. I heard Vic going out and opening. Voices. Vic called up to me, 'Harry, someone's asking for you.'

I went downstairs. Vic had gone back into his flat. A man waited in the porch. He said, 'Good evening, Mr Boas?'

He was no more than four-foot-nine high. He wore a smart summer overcoat buttoned tight across and a trilby hat. I said, 'I'm Boas. Who are you?'

I was looking over his shoulder at the Buick outside the gate. It was old, not too clean, and there were two people in it. He said politely, 'I've called on behalf of Mrs Humphrey.'

I didn't connect. 'Mrs Humphrey?'

'Mrs Humphrey. Of Half-Moon Street.' He was polite and attentive as an insurance salesman.

'Marcia!' I laughed. 'You had me for a minute. So who are you? The bailiffs?'

'We look after Mrs Humphrey's affairs. She was rather anxious about you. She thought there might have been some kind of accident.'

'No accident. I tried to ring her this morning.'

'I'm glad I called, then. It'll save you further trouble. If you'd kindly let me have the money, I'll give you a receipt.'

'How do I know who you are?'

He smiled politely. 'You know who we are.' There were two men in the car. One of them was sprawling behind the wheel. The other, in the back, was leaning forward to have a look at me through the window. They were both big fellows, in good suits. They both had the kind of hard, calm faces I have learned over many years to keep away from. He said, 'You can ring her. She's at home now. Or we'll be only too glad to take you to her.'

I said, 'Save yourself the trouble. I haven't got the money.'

He scratched his cheek thoughtfully. 'That's a pity. May I ask what has happened to it?'

'You may not. I'll tell her myself.'

'If you have the money, she'll be pleased to see you. Otherwise she leaves these matters entirely in our hands.'

'I'll deal direct.'

'No, Mr Boas. In future you'll be dealing with us. May I suggest you settle in seven days? We shan't call on you again till after that time. Goodnight, Mr Boas.'

Seven days. Such is my form.

CHAPTER NINETEEN

I stayed away from the factory next morning and went to Marcia's flat. The maid opened the door. She said, 'Madam thought you might call. She told me to ask if you had the money.'

'I'd like to talk to her.'

'Have you the money, sir?'

'Where is she?'

'Madam is not at home, sir. Have you brought the money?'

'No, I haven't.' She started to shut the door. I forced it open and pushed past her. Marcia was in her bedroom, sitting in front of her mirrors. She was rubbing some kind of cream into her face. She looked at me. The mask of cream had no expression, except for the glitter of the eyes. She turned back to the mirrors and said, 'Get out.'

'Marcia, let me tell you what happened.'

'I can guess what happened. Get out.'

'I tried to ring you yesterday. What's the idea, not letting me in?'

'I don't know you. It's too bad I ever did. I don't want to waste any more time on you. I pay money to have things like this looked after.'

'Marcia, I'll make it short. Give me time. That's all I'm asking. Just give me time. You'll get your money.'

'I'm sure I will. I made a great mistake trusting you. I don't propose to lose by it.' She turned to me, and the eyes without mercy gleamed at me again. 'Be careful, Boas. Very soon you might have a bad accident.'

'All right, I know you got protection. You don't have to put your strong-arm men on me.'

She was busy at the mirror again. 'I don't know what you're talking about.'

'Your goons called on me last night.'

'I've no idea what you mean. I'm just advising you to find that money quickly.' Her voice went very low and hard, and I glimpsed the anger against me behind that cold face. 'I don't like being made a fool of, Mr Boas.'

'Look, just give me a little time.'

'At one o'clock on Saturday you were due to give me a hundred and sixteen pounds. You're forty-seven hours late. Where's the money?'

'I'll get it for you—'

'I don't like giving forced loans. And I don't like scum pushing into my flat. You can get out now, and if you know what's good for you, you'll have that money double quick.'

'Just be patient, Marcia—'

'And wait till your luck changes? I've heard that old story. Nobody makes a fool of me. You'll have to learn that.'

'I can pay you in instalments. What's in it for you if I get smashed up?'

'Satisfaction.'

'One month. Just give me a month.'

'Boas, when anyone pushes my maid about, she knows where she has to phone for help. Someone should be here at any moment. I advise you to get out in good time.'

I went away.

*   *   *

I was pigsick with fright all that week. Whenever I came out of the house I looked up and down the street for the Buick. I swung out of bed every time the hollow bang of the doorknocker shook the house. Vic came upstairs one evening. Another frightened man. He had almost lost his voice with fear, and he croaked, staring at me, 'The auditors'll be in next week. What are you waiting for? For God's sake, I've only got till next week.'

I sat and looked at him, then all my anger burst out in a shout that stunned him. 'Then —ing well do something. Don't come to me. I'm fed up. Fed up.' I pushed him out of the room.

'Who am I? Your brother? You leave me alone.' I shut the door.

I had no time for Gregory, either. I was not in a mood to enjoy the charms of childhood. He came up a couple of times. I was short with him, and sent him packing, and he trotted downstairs looking cross and puzzled.

On Saturday I stayed in all day but in the evening I boosted myself with a pony of Scotch (an unusual need for me), dressed carefully and went to the dogs at White City.

I had tantalising luck. I won forty on the second race and perhaps you think I should have put it away. But money is to gamble with. In six more races forty can become four hundred. When you are desperate you see this as your only chance. The money was eked out by a couple of small wins but by the end of the evening most of it was gone.

I stayed in the bar after the last race and quietened my sick stomach with another double Scotch while the miserable mob trickled away.

In ten minutes the stadium was desolate. White programmes speckled the deserted terraces. The last handfuls of us walked down the stone steps and along concrete passages to the echo of our footsteps.

The two big fellows came into my path as if I had bumped into them in a fog, and when I looked over my shoulder the little one was behind me. He opened a door and a shove of two bodies sent me through it.

The door whooshed back into place. We were in a men's lavatory. Nobody was in there but us. It was full of a stale reek. The two big men had me backed up to a wall.

The little man said, 'Seven days, Mr Boas.'

'Lay off,' I said. 'I told her I'd pay.'

'Of course you'll pay.' He held out his hand.

'I'll pay in my time.'

'Mr Boas,' the little man said. The big ones were up against me like a couple of stone buttresses. Footsteps sounded in the corridor outside but no one came in. 'Have you ever seen a man who's been gone over? It's not a question of black eyes, you know. The human body is very sensitive. The spine, for example, or the kidneys. I heard of one man who was paralysed for life by a kicking. Another one is an imbecile. His mother looks after him. Have you got a mother, Mr Boas?'

I started to get a word out but he spoke over me. 'We'll call on you in the week. For the last time.'

He put the palm of his hand on my chest and pushed me back against the foul, wet tiles. He said, 'You've spoiled your coat.'

He jerked his head, and the three of them walked out.

*　　　　*　　　　*

Where do you run when you are frightened? Where does a small boy run?

I stopped a cab before I knew what I meant to do, and I gave Debbie's address. I sat back in the cab. My forehead was chill and clammy. My heart beat fast.

It was not ten o'clock yet. The cab could cut through to the North Circular and with luck I could be at Debbie's in a half-hour.

For once I could not make a plan. Could I tell her the truth? Could I tell her a lie?

I paid off the cab at the corner of her road and prowled past the house like a burglar. No cars stood outside. The curtains were drawn. A glow of light came through the windows of the downstairs lounge, and another from the front bedroom above. They had no company then, and thank God they were not all asleep. But who had gone up to bed? Who was downstairs? Would Gus or one of the girls open the door to me?

I touched the bell as lightly as I could. An inside door opened. My heart sang thanks at the sound of footsteps I knew. Debbie opened the door.

'Harry?' she said. I walked past her and she followed me into the lounge. 'You're late. Is everything all right?'

'Sure.'

'I've been looking at TV. Gus had an early night. Let me make you something to eat.'

'That's all right, Deb. How are you all?'

'We're fine. The girls are out. They enjoy life. Something on a tray? A glass of milk? Are you sure you're all right?'

'I'm lovely.'

'So sit down. Take your coat off.'

'I can't stay. Deb, I got a business worry. You know you offered to advance me money once?'

'Money?'

I didn't answer, but she gave a child's silent gasp and looked down at her hand. She was wearing the solitaire.

'I need some money in a hurry, Deb.'

'This is why you came so late at night?'

'It's not so late. I was round here, so I dropped in.'

'You need money? I'll call Gus down?'

'I asked Gus.'

She was silent. Then, 'Harryboy, what have I got except the housekeeping? The bills Gus pays.'

I looked at the ring. Her face was terrified. She said, 'It can't wait?'

'No.'

'You're in trouble?'

I didn't answer.

'Harry, you're in trouble. You wouldn't come here eleven o'clock at night if you weren't. What has happened? Tell me.'

'Debbie, don't ask me for a kaddish. It won't help. I need money. At once.'

She cried, 'What have you done? Harry, always you were such a good boy. Have you done something wrong?'

'Nothing wrong. Believe me. Deb, once upon a time you tried to give me something.'

'I must have had a dybbuk in me.'

'You mean you won't.'

'I'm frightened, Harryboy. How can I rob my husband? I love him. I don't know how to tell a lie. If I lie to Gus, if I lie to the insurance, they'll see the truth in my face.'

'Just to buy me a business you were ready to do it. This is more important.'

She wailed, 'You're in trouble, I know.' She started to twist the ring off her finger. 'I know you, if it wasn't some terrible trouble you wouldn't ask me. Here—' She held out the ring. 'Take. Quickly. Go away.'

The door opened. Gus was there in a dressing-gown. He said, 'My wife you make a thief.'

She cried, 'Gus—'

'All right.' The little man spoke as stern and deep as Isaiah. 'You know what your sister is? A good woman. A wonderful mother. A queen. A blessing on my life.'

Debbie was crying quietly.

He said, 'She couldn't do a sin if she tried, my Debbie. But you, you filth, you rottenness, you can take advantage, you can use her, you can twist her—'

She cried out, 'Gus, he's in trouble.'

He shouted at her, 'He makes you suffer. He makes you cry. You think it doesn't break my heart to see you cry?'

'He's my brother.'

'Go upstairs.'

She wept. 'He's in some trouble. I can tell it.'

'Go upstairs.'

She didn't move.

'Debbie, upstairs.'

She went. When the door had closed behind her, he said to me, 'Now I can say what I think of you without sticking knives in her heart. I curse you. You hear? I curse you for the unhappiness you bring on my wife. May you lie in the earth dead.'

'All right, Gus. You know it was all my fault.'

'I need you to tell me? Thank you. My Debbie needs no excuses. You were the thief. You. Misery you bring us. When she suffers, I suffer. So now you'll please get out? I tell you now, don't come here again. Leave your sister alone. You hear me?' He crossed and opened the door. I went into the hall.

He said harshly, 'What is this trouble?'

'If I don't pay someone I'll get smashed up.'

'What you deserve,' he said. 'What you deserve. Every bone in your body should be smashed.'

I opened the door.

He said, 'How much?'

I was going to name the right amount. There was a twitch in my mind, and I said, 'Two hundred.'

'Wait.'

He went into a back room. I waited.

He came out. A roll of notes was in his hand. He was breathing hard. His voice shook in the effort to speak calmly. 'Only for her. Only for my wife I do this.'

He held out the roll.

Then he choked, and flung it out of the door to drop on the garden path. I walked out and stooped to pick it up. As he closed the door, he said, 'Finished. The last time. You will never come to this house again.'

I was afraid to keep the money in case I changed my mind. I got home by half-past eleven. Evelyn and the kid were asleep but Vic was still studying in the back room. When he opened the door and I saw that he was alone, I gave him the roll of notes without a word.

He took it. He let his head fall back against the doorpost, his eyes closed for a moment and the breath sighed out of him. He opened his eyes and said, 'You took your time, didn't you?'

I turned and walked away.

'Harry.' He had followed to the foot of the staircase and he spoke softly for fear of waking Evelyn. 'I didn't know what I was saying. I've been out of my mind. I don't know how to thank you. I dare not think what you've saved me from.'

I said, 'Goodnight,' and went upstairs.

I'd saved him. What about me?

*   *   *

I was a demoralised man. It was a bad way to be. Once in the war a young lad who had gone to pieces told me bitterly that I didn't know what it was like. He had to keep forcing himself to live through one more hour, and each hour seemed an age.

This was how my days went by. The terror of enemies you can't see weighs a ton. You ache. You are dog tired. I didn't go to the track. I couldn't read. I lay on my bed, drank Scotch and smoked cheroots. My room stank with tobacco smoke, acrid like the smell of fear.

It was just before half-past eight on the Thursday night when from down the street I heard the slam of a car door. I sat up, as I did whenever I heard that sound now. My heart was thumping. Someone walked up to the front door and knocked. I was already on the landing in my socks, and I crept quickly down to the middle landing, slipping into the bathroom.

Another knock. Footsteps in the hall. The front door was opened.

Vic's voice, 'Good evening.'

A girl's voice. I didn't recognise it. It flipped me. 'Good evening. Is Mr Boas at home, please?'

'Just a moment, I'll see.' Vic came to the foot of the stairs and called, 'Harry!' A moment later, 'Harry!' He came up to the landing. From outside my door he called upstairs. 'Harry, there's someone to see you.'

He went up to my room. He came down to the landing and knocked on the lavatory door, next to mine. 'Are you in there, Harry?'

I waited. He must have seen that it was dark inside the bathroom. He went downstairs. At the street door, 'He must have just gone out. His room's full of smoke. It's funny, I didn't hear him go.'

'Oh, never mind.'

'Would you like to wait?'

'No, I'll call again later.'

'What name shall I say?'

'Never mind, I'll call again.'

She went down the steps. Vic closed the door and went into his back room. I slipped upstairs. The hunt was on. What could I do? There was no phone in the house. I would have to go out some time. Some time, they had to catch up with me. Who was the girl?

No light came from under the door of the Pole's room. The door was locked. I had to get a look at the street, and my room was at the back. Thank heavens for Joe de Souza's well-greased pulley. I opened the skylight cautiously and crept up on to the roof. It was dark, an October night. I crossed the leads and peeped over the parapet.

The car was parked about twenty yards from the house, away from the High Street, where the street was darker. The High Street on the other side was a shimmer of bright light, with the windows of all the closed shops kept illuminated till midnight. The girl was talking in through the front window of the car. Then she went away. I watched her turn into the bright, deserted High Street. A few moments later she went past on the platform of a bus. She was out of it now, a nobody, a stooge, brought along to ask at the door. The three men were not going to let any witness see them before the event.

The car waited.

I went back to my room. My head was packed with dizziness. I had only one instinct, to hide. Under the bed if possible. But that was no use. I could send Vic for the police, but when they came the car would just slide away into the night, and the men would catch up with me another time. All right, so run. This was the next thought, more than a thought, it split my head like sheet lightning. I didn't even think where.

First, to get out of the house quietly. I put on a light overcoat and a pair of rubber-soled shoes. I crept down the stairs. It took me minutes to pass Vic's room without making any floorboards creak. At the back of the house was a door into the garden. It was left open during the day so that people could put out rubbish and lumber (and such things as a tricycle of Gregory's). I was lucky again. The burglar-crazy Siskin had not yet done his evening round to fasten all the bolts. I let myself out.

The garden is a waste of weeds. All the back gardens of these tenements are rubbish dumps and jungles of weed. Low walls separate them, which give easy thoroughfare to dogs and cats. No one comes out after dark, and the fall of a dustbin lid is attributed to the nosing of a moggy.

I went over the back wall, going in the direction of the parked car. I went on, from garden to garden. From the houses, voices, the clatter of washing-up, the sound of the same television programme from one house to the next. Here and there light glared from a window without curtains, and people passed to and fro in the rooms, but no one saw me. I went to the last house of the Terrace. Then I let myself out by the side passage. I was in the street. Fifty yards behind the parked car. The men sat in the car, watching my house, their backs to me. I went down the street, turned off to the right, and another turn brought me to the bright lights and empty pavement of the High Street.

Now what? There is a bus stop near the corner of the street. I could swing on to a bus and be away in no time. But what then? Could I leave town without money? Could I come home to sleep? Could I go to the tracks and try and win enough for a getaway? Could I even go to the factory to earn myself a stake? I could run about all night. That was all I could do. They had me trapped.

I felt nervous on the wide pavement. There is a shop doorway on the street corner, deep and dark. I stepped into it. The shop has windows on both sides so that I could see through, down the Terrace, to the car parked beyond my house. I stood there, not knowing where to move next. I thought of that poem by John Masefield I used to like when a boy, of the fox pausing under a bush, his flanks heaving, smelling the reek of his hunters on the air.

I stood in the doorway. The men sat in the car. I began to feel cold. And with the cold, calm. Your fear gathers till it is a big lump in the throat. There comes a point where you cannot stand this lump any longer. Sooner than choke, you swallow and say, 'Enough,' and suddenly the lump is not there any more. You are not frightened any more.

My head was clear and my mind was working. Man is a hunting animal. I learned that in the war. (I was a bad boy in the Army, too much of an individualist, I took holidays whenever I fancied, but once they had shipped me overseas they had no more trouble with me.) I learned in the war with what incredible speed and clarity the mind can work when it's a matter of self-preservation. Plans were flashing in my head like a series of spot commercials on television. Get them on to your own ground. That was the rule for the fox. That was the rule of war. Get them on to the terrain that you know and they don't, that helps you and hinders them. It was no use running away from this bunch. They would only catch me in the end. As well to turn on them. I had to deal with them—somehow—tonight. What had I got to lose? The instinct of the trapped rat is sound. I had spent my boyhood in these streets. These men were foreigners, they had come from the West End, and to them the back streets of the borough were a wilderness, a maze in the night.

When fear goes, no warmth of courage takes its place. You just feel cool and light and clear-headed. You are as intent, poised and capable of split-second timing as a wild animal, your brain works like a computer, you are a functioning apparatus.

So here goes, Harryboy Boas! Who is the hunter and who is the quarry? You don't even know. But the calculations, the plans are racing through your mind, you are alert and ready.

I looked back down the High Street. I needed a bus. There were plenty of them running. I waited till I saw one just pulling away from the next stop. I calculated how long it would take him to reach the stop near me. I stepped out of the doorway, turned the corner and walked smartly down the street, Harryboy Boas coming back as expected, maybe from the tobacconist's, all unawares, walking into the trap.

I walked down the street, towards my house, towards the waiting car. The small white face under the trilby hat perked up. The little man had seen me. The car's engine started. I hesitated, as if I had just seen them, turned, and ran back towards the High Street.

I heard the surge of the engine as the Buick accelerated, but I had the operation timed to a second, and I was round the corner, and hurtling across the pavement as the bus started to pull away from the empty stop. Try to teach a London boy anything about jumping buses! I have put on weight and lost wind these last years, but the muscle, the know-how, the reflexes are still there. I flew on to the rear platform like a cat jumping with all four limbs, and we sped past the street corner as the Buick paused there. The little man pointed and the car turned into the main road, and cruised just behind us.

Well, it was deadlock for a little while. At every stop, people got on. My friends in the car couldn't very well come and take me off the bus. On the other hand, if I got off, there they were, sitting neatly behind the bus, keeping the same six-yard distance all the time. It must look to them as if they only had to wait. Each time the bus stopped, they stopped, ready to pick me up.

I sat on the rear bench of the bus and watched them through the back platform window. With an interest as unconcealed as my own the little man watched me through the windscreen of the Buick.

I was quite relaxed. Fears, terrors, perplexities, guilts, all the burdens of our life—they are all smoothed away by action. My mind was only concerned with action and it was ticking like a watch. Man is a hunter.

We were coming into a more crowded part of the main road, where it becomes the Kingsland High Street. People thickened on the pavement, groups of boys and girls singing and yoo-hooing, people coming out of cinemas, the last stalls packing up in Ridley Road market and the last shoppers coming away, and the groups thickening into crowds as we neared the busiest crossroads in this part of London, Dalston Junction.

For my purposes, it didn't matter which way the traffic lights went at the Junction. In fact they were at red. The bus pulled up against a pavement thickly crowded, and without any warning to my pursuers I swung by the handrail straight round from my seat, off the platform and on to the pavement, slipping away into the crowd. Let them try to touch me in the middle of this mob. I didn't look back to see how they were coping with the problem of the crowd and of the traffic lights. I darted through the crowd and round the corner into Dalston Lane. The buses come down here almost in convoy. A few blocks up they separate, some following the curve of Dalston Lane and some going up Graham Road. Once again, either way suited me. I had chosen my ground.

I jumped a bus and took a seat near the back. It lumbered fifty yards down Dalston Lane and pulled in at the bus stop. I didn't want to lose my friends. I was glad to see their car come round the corner while people poured on to the bus. I was also glad that there was a long queue at the stop, which filled the bus. The one thing I had feared was that one of the three men—one only would have been enough—would have nipped on to the bus and sat down calmly next to me.

We went along Dalston Lane, past the police station, crossed the lights and continued along Graham Road. I watched for the railway bridge ahead of me. There was no bus stop on this stretch, the bus hit a good speed and the car sped behind. We came alongside a high fence. Once more I grasped the rail, swung round and dropped off the bus fast, the way I had been taught to drop off fast-moving trucks in the Army. I kept running, only five paces across the pavement, hearing the screech of the Buick's brakes right behind me—and I was in, running, through high white wooden gates.

This was my chosen ground. I was in the railway goods and coal yard.

I had no plan, only to get them out of their car and if possible separated. As I ran into the dark wilderness of rails and trucks and black coal bunkers, with a grass embankment and the tracks of the overhead electric railway looming above me on my right, I heard the car run into the yard, the doors open, and the men's running footfall.

This was my terrain. For a mile around, whichever bus I had jumped, I would have landed into this area, where some railway tracks run through deep cuttings and meet as mazes of rails in wide, desolate goods yards. Another railway line runs overhead on a series of bridges, narrow alleys where a car cannot pass run alongside the railway arches, dozens of turnings are blind alleys, ending at the railway. At a dozen points I could have got the three out of their car and scattering to chase me, in a darkness friendly to me. I had hunted and been hunted here as a boy, when it was gang against gang. I knew every inch of the ground. And here, now, I was being hunted—and hunting—again.

Here and there an overhead light glimmered. No one seemed to be about. If anyone had been, I need only have led my pursuers on from yard to yard, from one railway arch to another, till we reached a lonely enough place. But here it was empty, silent, the gates left open for some late, last lorry to come in and park.

So I heard the car pull up, and my hunters spill out in the second it stopped, and their shoes running over the broken asphalt, and I dodged fast, circling clockwise, from wagons to coal heaps, until I was back near the entrance, where the Buick stood, its left-hand doors wide open, as its occupants vanished into the shadows in search of me.

On silent shoes I stepped across to the car and slipped into the front seat. My luck held. They had tumbled out so fast that the key was still in the ignition. I sat comfortably and watched.

One of the big men came out from behind a wagon. A few moments later, the other joined him. They walked towards me, looking into the bays and the recesses on their left formed by huts and bunkers against the railway embankment.

Only two. Never mind. They were a few yards away when I switched on the motor and, lights still off, stepped hard on the gas pedal. The open doors slammed with the shock of the take-off. The two men scattered apart and I went through between them. I felt the impact on my wings and they flew apart. Only one of them cried out. I jammed on brakes and jumped out of the car. They both lay crookedly on the ground, about ten yards apart. One of them was moving and groaning.

The little man came out from behind a wagon, saw me and vanished again. I went in among the wagons after him.

I had been ready to swerve and only catch the two big fellows a glancing blow. I felt like killing, but I had no intention of getting into that sort of a mess. As it was, their running apart had given me just what I wanted. There would be some broken bones back there on the ground, but nothing worse.

The road outside is a quiet one, no shops, just old, dark houses, and no one seemed to have been attracted by the brief noises in the yard.

I hunted the little man among the trucks. I had better not underestimate him. He was probably the kind who could use himself scientifically. Of a gun I had no fear, but he might even carry that tool of a vanishing craft, a razor.

I saw him first. I came up behind him, almost silent, pinned him with my body to a wagon before he could turn, knocked his hat off, grabbed his hair and began to bash his head against the side of the wagon like a kid trying to crack a coconut. Now I wanted to kill, wanted it badly. Man is a killer. I learned that in the war. It is all nuts about conscience. In Normandy I was with a bunch of steady, ordinary boys from respectable homes, craftsmen, clerks, ordinary boys, and they killed men like killing rabbits. Years after, I went to a reunion, and over pints of beer I heard quiet, ordinary fellows, a greengrocer, a waiter, a shipping clerk, chuckle with contentment and pride over their memories of this killing and that killing. So I bashed his head against the hinges on the truck, and even while he was conscious he made no sound louder than grunt-grunt-grunt, and the lust to kill swelled my muscles hard in my sleeves like the lust for a woman swells you hard in your trousers. But I held myself in, my mind was still ticking like a machine, not too much, not too much, not too much, and as soon as he sagged limp I forced myself to stop—it was an ache making myself stop—and I let him down to the ground.

I stooped over him, undid his overcoat with my gloved fingertips and felt under his jacket. He was breathing all right. His forehead was laid open and the blood was all down his face. My hand, as it came away, felt a wallet. I took the wallet. This was the first time in my life I had stolen, except for looting the enemy in war, and this felt the same.

Beyond the trucks I could hear voices, footsteps round the Buick. The groaning must have attracted someone.

There was no other gate to the yard. But I didn't have to go out that way. I had played here as a kid. Once again, as when I was twelve years old, I crossed to a coal bunker at the foot of the embankment, and ran up the mound of coal that was stacked almost to the top of the brick wall of the railway. I dropped the ten feet on the other side of the wall as lightly as if I had kept in practice all these years, and went at a shallow diagonal run up the grass embankment.

This took me up alongside the track. I crossed the bridge over the railway cutting. On the far side, as I remembered from boyhood, was the old flight of steps down from the bridge to another yard, another lorry park. The railway people hadn't even put the usual few strands of barbed wire across the bottom.

A minute later I was in a dark, back street again. I peeled off my gloves, which had blood on the fingertips, dropped them next to an open drain, took a wad of notes from the wallet, dropped the wallet, then used my shoe to push gloves and wallet down the drain.

A few hundred yards brought me out into Dalston Lane, at the far end. I felt exhilarated. Full of energy. It was only a short, straight bus ride from here to the Clapton dog track, and the thing seemed fated. In the same exalted mood I got to the track. Not much time had passed since I slipped out of the back of my house. They were just parading the dogs for the seventh race.

Without hesitation, without thought, with utter certainty, filled with a giant's strength, I put all the little man's money on a two-year-old bitch called Tinkerbell.

A man's luck has to change some time. It is all a question of keeping on long enough. I walked out of the track with two hundred and sixty pounds in my pocket.

CHAPTER TWENTY-ONE

Eleven o'clock next morning I was ringing Marcia's doorbell. The maid tried to shut the door when she saw me, but I showed her my fat wallet and she let me in. I waited in the lounge. After a while Marcia came in, looking as distinguished as ever in a maroon housecoat of corduroy velvet.

She stood easily in the doorway, looking me over with cool eyes as if I was an item in a shop window. I put a wad of notes on the table and said, 'A hundred and sixteen pounds.'

She said nothing. She kept her arms crossed, stroking her own shoulders as if she was cold, her lips pursed. I put another wad alongside the first. She said, 'What's that?'

'Interest. A hundred.'

'You've become very liberal all of a sudden.'

'It's self-interest. I thought it might pay off your friends.'

She went across to a liquor cabinet and with her back to me began to handle glasses and bottles, 'What friends?'

'Didn't you hear about your three friends in the Buick? They had an accident last night.' She was coming across to me with a glass of Scotch. 'I don't suppose it would get in the national papers.'

'I don't read the papers,' she said. She gave me the glass. 'Three, did you say? I begin to think you're a man of quality, Harry.'

'Anyway,' I said, 'I don't want a feud on my hands. Call them off.'

'I really don't know what you're talking about.'

'Maybe you don't. But you've got your money now, Marcia. I don't want any more trouble.'

'I shouldn't worry if I were you.'

'I'd like to be sure.'

She picked up both bundles of notes. 'You can be sure.'

'Quite sure?'

'Quite sure.'

'You know the guy who gives the orders, do you?'

'What orders?' Points of mockery made a smile in her eyes.

'All right, you know the guy,'

'I know a lot of guys.'

'Well,' I said, putting down my empty glass and getting up. 'I must run along. No hard feelings, Marcia.'

'Come again,' she said, 'when you can afford it.'

*   *   *

I had over forty pounds left, I had broken my bad luck, Vic's ton of misery was off my shoulders, the villains would bother me no more, and it was a cold, clear morning. I walked through the West End lightly. In those last days of October, the children were getting ready for Guy Fawkes' Night, and cheeky little clusters of Cockney kids were everywhere collecting for fireworks, with their guys on display. 'Penny for the guy!' 'Penny for the guy, mister.' I was the Aga Khan that morning. I made myself drunk with the lordly joy of giving money away. I left behind me a string of happy kids gaping at the shillings and half-crowns I had given them.

I had a fat Italian lunch with wine, I took in a film in the afternoon, and, a lord to the last, I picked up a cab for the long drive home to Hackney.

All was right with my world. I walked into the house. I could hear Gregory playing on the floor in the front bedroom, singing one of his mysterious, wordless incantations. I knocked at the door of the back room and went in gaily. Vic was already setting out some of his books, for a half-hour's work while he waited for his supper. His coming-home pot of tea was still on the table, and Evelyn was finishing her cup. I said, 'Hallo,' to both of them, and to Vic, 'All well?'

He said, 'Yes, thank you.' There was something smothered and evasive in his voice that puzzled me, and his eyes kept guiltily away from me. Evelyn had not answered me. She gave me a strange, black look, got up and went out to the kitchen, where she looked into saucepans with an odd, demonstrative banging of their lids.

Alone with Vic, I dropped a hand on his shoulder. 'Got it all fixed up safe?'

'Everything's OK.' He made an embarrassed squirming movement to get away from my hand. 'Thank you.'

'You don't have to keep saying thank you. Just forget it.'

'Oh—' And again there was a mysterious note in his voice, desperate and derisive—'I shan't do that. I'm very grateful. I am, I assure you. I shall always feel under an obligation.'

I was puzzled, but I couldn't very well ask what was wrong because of a few strange words and looks. I said, 'What about a cup of tea?'

I saw his hesitation. Then, with a jaunty bitterness, 'All right.'

Without speaking, and uncomfortable because he felt me watching him, he poured a cup of tea from the used pot, getting the dregs out without troubling to put in fresh water, and set the cup in front of me. There was something childish about all these strange, defiant actions. He sat at the table and ostentatiously opened one of his books.

I said, 'Look, what is this, Vic?'

He did not look up. 'Do you mind, Harry? I want to do some work before supper.'

'What is this? What's happened?'

'Nothing. I said thank you. I'm very grateful for all you've done.'

'Exactly what has he done?' This was Evelyn, from the kitchen. 'What have you got to thank him about? I'm fed up with all this kow-towing to him.' She stood there full of hate, and I was more mystified than ever. I said to Vic, 'Is everything all right?' He didn't answer. 'Has somebody gone crazy?'

Silence. I turned to the door, and if he had let me go, it would all have ended there, in mystery. But he couldn't hold himself in, and he cried out, 'Just because you do me a favour, it doesn't give you the right to make a pass at my wife.'

I stopped. The room was silent. I looked at Evelyn. She looked back at me defiantly, her mouth clamped.

'What favour?' she said. 'What's all these favours he's done you?'

I was looking at Vic now. He dared not look back at me. I said, 'Did she tell you that?'

He muttered, 'I don't know what I'm going to do now. We'll have to move now.'

I said, 'I see.'

He burst out, 'Haven't you got enough women? Did you have to try and take my wife away?'

'Take your wife?' I looked at her. I couldn't help it. I laughed out loud.

'You chaps who run after women are all the same. You can be straight about everything else, but with women you just think you can help yourself, whoever they are.'

I was too sick, too tired to stay in the absurd situation any more. I moved to the door. 'All right,' I said, 'all right.'

Evelyn had been standing in the kitchen doorway, quivering with the derisive laugh I had given her. She said, hard and loud as a trumpet, 'And don't come back. Keep away from us.'

'Don't worry,' I said. 'I will. You've told your husband a story. Maybe he'll tell you one some time.'

Vic was staring at his book, fear printed on his face. I was so full of hate myself that I had to needle him. 'I see you haven't told your wife that story,' I said. 'You ought to, some time. She'll laugh herself silly.'

Evelyn said, 'What story?'

Without raising his eyes Vic muttered, 'I'm sorry, Harry.'

Evelyn sounded off like a trumpet again. 'What are you sorry about? Why are you always so humble to this man? I've told you what he tried to do to me. Is that all you can say, you're sorry? We could go to the police after what he did.' She turned on me. 'Do you realise we could go to the police?'

I grinned at Vic. 'Oh, your husband wouldn't do that.'

She grew shrill. 'You're so clever. You think you own the world. You all do. All of you. You're laughing at us. It makes me sick, it makes me feel dirty just to think of what you wanted me to do. You expected me to do that with you? With the likes of you?'

I said to Vic, 'Take her to a psychiatrist.'

She cried, 'And leave the child alone. God, when I think I've trusted him up there with you—'

'That's enough from you,' I said. 'You make me sick. The pair of you. You—' I was talking to Evelyn—'you rotten snivelling little snob. You've got nothing, nothing, all you live on is hatred for other people. That's not flesh on your bones. It's envy. You're made of envy. If you believe—' this was to Vic—'I could want her, you'll believe anything. I've got no pity for you. You get what you deserve. If you had any backbone you'd have had her fixed long ago. For a year now I've had you all round my neck—all of you— the kid's as bad as you are. He hasn't given me a minute's peace since you came here. You think I want him stampeding up my stairs every day, making himself at home in my room? I can't call a minute of my life my own.' I was furious now, against the kid as much as his parents. All the irritation I had felt with him when he came upstairs pestering me in this past week thickened in my voice. 'He's worse than you two, he is. As far as he's concerned, I'm a machine for playing games with, installed on the top floor. Well, I don't want him, do you hear me? I don't want him smooching over me with his grubby hands and his wet kisses. Keep away from me. All of you. The three of you. If you don't like me, then move. I'm comfortable here. I'm not gonna move, you know. I've lived here for years, I'm comfortable. You move. You—' to Vic—'you want to move? Get some money. Rob the cashbox or something. It's been done. You won't get into trouble, someone'll help you out. Only leave me alone. From now on. All of you.'

I went out, and up to my room.

Now, during this wretched scene, something had happened which none of us had noticed. Gregory had come in quietly. Perhaps the noise of our voices had attracted him. He had stood in the doorway behind me and listened to most of what was said. Then he had gone away again, quietly.

*   *   *

Ten minutes later I heard the explosion. Even from my room it sounded loud. And at once, after the explosion, the screaming. It took me seconds to react, till I realised that this was not a child's tantrum-screaming, but something desperate and terrible. And, almost at once, I heard the high, distracted voices of the parents.

I ran downstairs. They were in the bedroom. Evelyn sat on the bed, and she held Gregory on her lap, hugged close to her. His face was blackened and his eyes were clenched shut, and they looked like two little screwed-up knots of scorched skin. He was moaning now, very softly, and pressing his fists to his face, and I could see that they, too, were scorched. Vic babbled to me that he was going to phone, and he ran out of the house.

I said to Evelyn, 'Can I get water or something?'

She did not answer. She looked at me briefly, not with hatred any more, but without recognition, then began to comfort her child again, with tiny soft kisses on his head and his burned hands.

The room was full of an explosive reek. On the rug in front of the gas fire I saw a burned, splayed-open cylinder of cardboard. A firework casing. I did not bother Evelyn with questions. In a few minutes Vic came back. He muttered to me that the ambulance was coming.

I waited across the room, but Vic stayed close to his wife and child. From time to time he touched the child, tentatively, and tried to murmur some comfort, but the child ignored him. Gregory pressed close to his mother, as if he wanted to grow into part of her body again. It was like that other time, only complete, a final assertion of the unity of child and mother. Without stopping, very softly, very weakly, he moaned, 'Mummy, Mummy, Mummy—' She rocked him, her arms round him tenderly yet making a barrier against all the world, all the world including Vic, and she murmured to the child in a wonderfully soft, soothing, musical voice. She wrapped him in her warmth. She poured consolation into him. And he gave himself to her completely. The father hovered close by, but no one else existed but the mother and child, reunited now in utter perfection. So she guarded her child till the ambulance came.

Later, when the police had made their enquiries, we pieced together what had happened. The child had heard our quarrel—our stupid battering of each other with our own grown-up sickness. He had stood there, and watched the only three people who could give him any protection, any security, anything to trust, destroying in front of his eyes his picture of them. He had seen his parents quarrel before but now he had seen me, too, exposed. He had heard the things I said about him, and his child's unfailing ears had heard the note of truth, of hatred, in my voice. He had heard me reject him. And he had gone quietly out of the room, betrayed. Perhaps the second child I had betrayed.

He was a sturdy little child, not a child for tears but for making the best of it, for lifting up his little chin and marching on, alone if need be.

What he had done before he did again. While we quarrelled, hearing nothing outside ourselves, he dragged a chair to the street door, climbed on it, opened the door and went out.

In the street, in the gloom of a winter evening, he had found consolations, the whole world to stare at with big eyes. He had trotted up the street and stood humbly on the outskirts of a crowd of boys examining the fireworks they had bought with their Guy Fawkes money. In rapt wonderment he had watched the bigger boys light one or two Golden Fountains and Catherine Wheels experimentally.

And one of them, a kid hardly older than himself, six years old, had seen the little thing standing there, with such a forlorn, serious face, and to cheer him up, to make him feel one of the group, had taken a firework from the box and given it to him. It was a 'banger'.

Clutching the firework, Gregory had trotted home. His little mind, always so active and eager to find how things work, must have forgotten (for the moment) the ugly, wounding scene of the grown-ups. It was full of one thing only—to find out all about this wondrous, mysterious possession he clutched, this possession which made him a Big Boy, this firework.

And so he trotted back into the bedroom, where the gas fire burned behind its wire guard. He knew what he had to do. He had seen the big boys do it with the Catherine Wheel, holding the fireworks without fear. The fireguard had been no obstacle. In a minute he had unhooked one side and dragged it back. He knelt in front of the gas fire, and did what he had seen the big boys do—he put the blue fuse to the flame and lit it. Then, holding the firework proudly in front of him, close to his wondering eyes, he waited.

CHAPTER TWENTY-TWO

They let Evelyn stay by the bedside. Vic and I waited for her most of the night, walking the stone, tiled hospital corridors or the street outside.

The house doctor didn't tell us much. They never do. He said the kid had been treated for burns to the hands and face, and was coming along comfortably. He told us not to worry, and we went home.

They kept giving us these sunshine bulletins for two days, then they said that the kid's eyes were 'rather troublesome' and they were transferring him to the Eye Hospital where he could get specialist treatment.

It's the waiting that is awful when you are trying to get news from a hospital. You have to wait till this doctor comes on Monday, and that doctor comes on Thursday, and then you have to wait till you can get hold of them.

At last we got an explanation from the eye specialist. Gregory's eyes had been damaged by the firework. His hands and face were responding to the treatment for burns but the damage to his eyes was serious.

The left eye was the worst. The front of the eye was badly scorched by the burn. The transparent part, the cornea, was involved. Ulceration could result, and permanent opacity.

I was with Vic. I said, 'Opacity. You mean blindness?'

'Yes. In that eye.'

Vic said, 'What about the other eye?'

The doctor said he was more optimistic about that eye. Only a minor degree of damage had been incurred, and this was not over the central part of the cornea, but at the edge, which would not greatly reduce vision in that eye.

A question occurred to me but I did not ask it. I didn't want to terrify Vic. But Vic thought of it himself. He asked, 'If the child has only one functioning eye, and this is damaged, could that eye give out in time? I have heard of people with one eye going blind through the strain of it.'

The doctor said, in the careful way these people have, 'It would give rise to anxiety in the future.'

'You mean,' Vic said, 'he could be blind.'

The doctor told him not to fear something that might never happen. They were treating the eyes, and might yet save them both. If not, they could graft a new cornea on to the left eye and save it that way. There would certainly be no cause for worry about the right eye if it was one of two functioning eyes.

So we went home. Vic was saying all the way, 'He could be blind. My child could be blind.'

*   *   *

They have wonderful drugs these days. I kept telling Vic this, and he and Evelyn kept telling each other.

Gregory had to stay in hospital for over two months, till the inflammation in his eyes had died down, when the doctors could see what scarring had been left. He was treated with hydro-cortisone and antibiotics. But all through this time—ten weeks—they couldn't tell us anything.

His hands and face healed easily. He sat up in bed and greeted his visitors joyfully, and he looked his old self. Except for his eyes. The hospital people were wonderful to him. They always are to children these days. He played with marvellous toys his parents had never been able to afford. He munched sweets and chocolates happily. But he looked pathetic in dark glasses, and he would ask, in his small, querulous voice, why he couldn't see properly. We kept reassuring him that the doctor was to make him better, but he looked at us with a pathetic distrust—who can blame him after his experience of us?—and kept asking, 'When can I come home?'

Ten weeks. Looking at the child so small and unaware, always being politely told by the hospital people that it was too early for news. And wondering. Ten horrible weeks.

Christmas came and went. It meant nothing to me. The Deaners were to stay for a few days with Evelyn's parents but they could not enjoy themselves. Between them and me there was no hostility, no friendship, only a truce of unhappiness. We didn't talk much. When we did it was in muted voices, about the kid.

But in those ten weeks a lot happened to me. I went to the factory because the roar of the machines and the bray of music killed time. Some evenings I went to the dogs but I only dabbled. A lot of the time I just lay on my bed or walked around the dark streets. I have told you about this obsession I get sometimes, about a child of mine. I know it is silly. Just because I knocked about with a girl twenty-four years ago and I lost track of her, after all in most men's lives there are women they lost track of years ago—is there any reason why this bug should come into my mind from time to time? But it does, and it did in those ten weeks.

Maybe it is something personal that eats me, because I have no son. Maybe everybody should feel guilty that we live in a time when millions of children have been done to death, and it is just my bad luck that because of an incident in my life, I cannot forget like others do. You can forget a million children. You cannot forget one child.

I made excuses for myself. I said I had only done small acts of wrong, the kind everybody does. But the smallest acts, even of thoughtlessness, lead to the greatest of evils. It is the old, universal human excuse, 'I never meant any harm.' Perhaps when the species is no more, all the armies of human souls will wail that one excuse in front of the throne of the Almighty, 'We never meant any harm.'

*   *   *

In the New Year we got the verdict. Gregory's right eye had been saved. It would be weakened, but it would not fail if he had another eye to see with.

But he did not have another eye to see with. The left eye was blinded.

There was one resource left to save him from eventual total blindness. A corneal graft. They have a bank of corneas at the hospital. People leave them in their wills. Gregory could be given his sight back.

It only needed an operation.

But the delays, the agonies, were not over yet. The operation couldn't take place just yet. There had been an unprecedented run of operations recently. The 'eye bank' was empty. Gregory would have to wait.

*   *   *

Evelyn wept. Vic consoled her. It wouldn't be long, he said.

An idea was forming in me. An obsession. For hours every night I walked the streets and I thought about this idea. My whole life seemed to have led me to it. I couldn't get rid of it. Soon I didn't want to get rid of it. It burned in my head. It had become a need, a terrible need.

*   *   *

One day I went to the Eye Hospital. I asked to see the doctor in charge of the case. He knew me. He had seen me with Vic. After a bit of chit-chat, I said, 'You want an eye for this kid. You can have mine.'

He didn't answer. I said, 'What's the matter? Hasn't anyone given an eye before?'

'Yes,' he said. 'Yes, they have. As a matter of fact, only last year somebody did. A mother, for her son.'

I said, 'Well, then?'

He sat with his fingers laced on the desk in front of him, thinking. He said, 'The child only has to wait. We'll get a cornea in due course, and do the job.'

'When?'

'That I can't say.' He smiled. 'After Christmas seems to be a bad time of the year for many things.'

'I don't want any delay,' I said.

He said, 'Let me make something clear. We can't take your cornea without taking the eye.'

'This I understand.'

'You'll lose an eye.'

'So? By profession, doctor, I am a gambler. As long as I can read the Tote Board with my other eye, I got nothing to worry about.'

He started to rub his hand across his mouth.

I said, 'As a matter of fact, there's an old superstition that one-eyed men are lucky. In my game I need luck.'

He let himself smile properly. 'You're a bit of a joker, Mr Boas. But this is a serious matter. I don't see how I can do this.'

'Is there any law to stop you?'

'No.'

'Have you got any right to refuse?'

'Yes, I have the discretion to refuse.'

'Doctor, think of the kid. You're looking after him fine here, but set him free. Put him right, please, and set him free.'

He said, 'What do the parents think about this?'

'They don't know. I don't want them to.'

'I see.' I saw refusal hardening in his face.

I got up and stood over him. 'You don't see. Listen, doctor. Let me tell you something. You've seen the wife and the husband. All right—the husband's not the father. I am.'

He looked up at me.

I said, 'They mustn't know. You can see why, now. Neither of them must know. Is there any need for them to know?'

'It's not necessary.'

'Well, then?'

He was still silent.

'Listen,' I said. 'What is the alternative?'

'The child can go home,' he said. 'We shall send for him when we are ready.'

'Have you seen him?' I asked. 'Every time someone comes, he asks, "When can I come home?" Do you really want to send him home and then drag him back here again. What's it going to do to him?'

'There would be some emotional disturbance,' he said.

'Some?' I said. 'He'd be terrified, poor kid. And in the meantime, wearing those dark glasses, feeling himself different from other kids, wondering why we haven't kept our promise to make him better. Another grown-up promise. I don't want it,' I said. 'D'you hear, I don't want it.'

He didn't answer.

I said, 'This is his father talking to you. His father. A mother did it. They didn't say "No" to her. Why not a father?'

One thing I like about doctors is that they are business-like. They don't waste time on sentiment. He was silent for another few moments, then he pulled a chair across to the window and said, very briskly, 'I'll have to see if your eyes are healthy. Come and sit over here by the light.'

*   *   *

Now I felt fine. I was the hero of the big picture. One stroke was going to make everything right, all my life. God was good. With my eye a child would see. It is not hard for a man to do this kind of thing. I had a letter in my pocket telling me when to go into hospital. I walked around with springs in my heels. The air was sweet in my lungs.

I changed to another room. How could I let the Deaners see me with a black patch over my eye? Oh yes, I had it already figured. I dreamed of myself as the devil-may-care fellow with the black patch. Fashionable. A well-known figure at the tracks. I was already deciding what suits I'd buy to go with it. And I was sure, I was dead certain, that the eyepatch would bring me luck with the bookies. I tell you, every day my head and my heart swelled a bit more.

I left the house quietly. I did not even give the lamenting Siskin a forwarding address. Why make complications? And who should write me letters?

Once more I went to see the kid. The last time. You have to make a break. But this once I could not resist. After all, he would be asking for Harryboy and I had to explain to him that I would be going away for a while. He was sitting up in bed with toys all round him, and he was wearing dark glasses. When he lifted his little face up I went soft in the guts. Poor little blighter, I could see his problems rising up in front of him like the Himalayas. Well, he would just have to soldier on like the rest of us, alone. At least he would have two eyes to do it with. I kissed him on the head and left.

Came the great day, I swaggered into the hospital. I went into the office. I gave the letter to the reception girl and I said, 'Here I am, darling.'

She looked at the letter, and she looked at me, puzzled. She said, 'Didn't you get our telegram?'

'Telegram?'

'Telling you not to come.'

'Not to come?' I was Little Sir Echo this morning.

'We sent you a telegram three days ago.'

A pause, till I was able to speak. 'I changed my address.'

'I'm sorry, Mr Boas,' she said. 'I'm sorry you've been troubled like this. You must have had a lot of unnecessary anxiety.'

'Anxiety?' She should only know. I was oozing dismay. 'What about my eye?'

I must have said this indignantly because she stared at me. 'Your eye?' This echo lark was infectious.

'They wanted my eye for the kid. Gregory Deaner.'

'Oh.' She beamed at me. 'Bless you, Mr Boas, Gregory had his operation yesterday.'

'Yesterday?'

'He's fine. He's a great favourite, everyone here knows him. He'll be home in a few weeks.'

'But—' My hand went up to my eye.

'Oh heavens—' She was a nice-looking young bit. Her smile was joyful. 'We shouldn't have taken yours except as an absolutely last resort. It never takes long for a cornea to come into the eye bank. We've been phoning all over the country. It's all right, Mr Boas, you can go home with a light heart.'

'What is this?' I must have bellowed this, because her eyes opened like pennies in surprise. 'Where's this doctor I saw?'

But against his name on the board was a slide with the word OUT.

She said, 'What do you want to see the doctor for?'

I was struck dumb. What did I want to see him for? Could I scream at him, 'You can't do this to me'?

No, we don't get let off so easy. What a laugh! I said, 'The kid's all right, is he?'

'He'll be fine. I could arrange for you to have just a peep at him.'

'No. Not just now.'

I went home. I felt like the bride in the song who was left waiting at the church. Such is my form. Always.

*   *   *

So here I am, Harryboy Boas, back where I started from. I have lost my snug room. I have fallen out with my brother-in-law. And my great gesture fell as flat as all my other great plans.

Never mind. In my new room there is no one to bother me. I can read. And after all, you should never give up hope before the dogs have crossed the finishing-line.

THE END

From the City, From the Plough

Alexander Baron

introduction by Sean Longden

The story of soldiers of the Fifth Battalion, the Wessex Regiment in the run up to and after D-Day. Although fictional, it comes directly out of the author's own experience, and is one of the most accurate and unsentimental portrayals of the ordinary soldier's life anywhere in fiction. The prose is spare and crisp, the narrative voice at times chilling, but alive to the humour and humanity of soldiers at war as well as the conflict's ruthlessness and inhuman momentum.

"This is the only war book that has conveyed any sense of reality to me"
V. S. PRITCHETT

"robust and honest without being sensational, warm-hearted without being sentimental, stimulating without being slick"
NEW STATESMAN

"Every scene is alive with humour and pity, with a deep controlled fury, with the stuff of life itself...tough, taut, yet profoundly expressive...This book left me mentally numb for a week...Get this book and read it...insist on having it...it is magnificent"
TRIBUNE

"A war book that is the real thing"
DAILY TELEGRAPH

"A fine and moving book"
NEW YORK TIMES

Black Spring Press • paperback • 978-0-948238-44-4 • 224pp

King Dido

Alexander Baron

introduction by Ken Worpole

1911, East London. The police collaborate with racketeers to keep
an uneasy peace, periodically broken by vicious street wars. Dido
Peach comes to prominence running protection rackets by breaking
the unwritten rules of the underworld. His fall is just as spectacular,
shaking even the callous and vicious world he lived in.

"Enthralling"
   SUNDAY TIMES

*"Alexander Baron was a skilled traditionalist, a contriver of plotdriven,
socially perceptive meditations on place."*
   IAIN SINCLAIR

New London Editions • paperback • 978-1-905512-81-2 • 360pp

Rosie Hogarth

Alexander Baron

introduction by Andrew Whitehead

In the spring of 1949, Jack Agass belatedly returns from the war to
the working-class street in Islington where he grew up. A proud,
supportive community—with a pub and a barber shop, and a
common love of the Arsenal. But the street has changed. Jack
eventually finds his footing but he's haunted by a yearning for his
old childhood friend Rosie Hogarth, and for the pre-war security
and certainties she represents. Rosie has moved out and up—living
bohemian-style in Bloomsbury. He thinks she's selling sex—it turns
out her motive is political.

A taut and very human drama is played out through the summer
and autumn of the year. In his first London novel, Alexander Baron
provides one of the most powerful and compassionate evocations of
a working-class community in the throes of profound change.

New London Editions • paperback • 978-1-905512-98-0 • 105pp